The Rajapaksa Stories

Dear Ann & Dave,

It's been great getting to know you over the last year. Hope you enjoy the book

— Koom

The Rajapaksa Stories

by Koom Kankesan

with Introduction and Recipes
by Ma Rajapaksa

LYRICALMYRICAL

The publication of *The Rajapaksa Stories* has been generously supported by the Canada Council for the Arts and the Ontario Arts Council.

Canada Council for the Arts / Conseil des Arts du Canada

ONTARIO ARTS COUNCIL / CONSEIL DES ARTS DE L'ONTARIO
50 YEARS OF ONTARIO GOVERNMENT SUPPORT OF THE ARTS
50 ANS DE SOUTIEN DU GOUVERNEMENT DE L'ONTARIO AUX ARTS

Author's photograph: Anne
Cover design: Sarah Beaudin
Editor: Luciano Iacobelli

Typography: bellina works

Library and Archives Canada Cataloguing in Publication

Kankesan, Koom

The Rajapaksa stories / Koom Kankesan.

Short stories.

ISBN 978-1-897275-75-7

I. Title.

PS8621.A55R33 2013   C813'.6   C2013-900925-6

Published by Lyricalmyrical Books
Toronto, Ontario
www.lyricalmyricalpress.com
Printed in Canada

to Alan Moore,
for mind and morals

Contents

Introduction

Acknowledgements

Introduction
by Ma Rajapaksa

Well, I'm surprised they asked me to write this introduction, mostly because I'm the mother of the man in question: Mahinda Rajapaksa. The president of Sri Lanka, our glorious leader. Conqueror, lawgiver, erstwhile movie star! My son, Mahinda. My darling Mahinda, the prince of my life! He gave up his early dreams of starring in the movies to star in the country's political future. Almost singlehandedly, he took the country forward to a bold new epoch, crushing the rebels, freeing the people from the grip of civil war.

The other reason I'm surprised is that I'm dead. I died years ago. They had to hire a Sri Lankan medium to contact my spirit and write down these words from the other side. Well, I'm happy to do it because I need a break, and I'm actually hiding out from my husband, Mahinda's father and former politician: Don Alvin Rajapaksa. Known to most as D. A.

We have a saying in Hambantota where we once lived: the profession may be *medium* but the fee is quite *large*. So, if there are any problems with this introduction, you *can* blame the messenger. You can even 'shoot' him if you want. Of course, not without blame is the lazy writer of this poor tome (I hear he is unemployed and has an unhealthy addiction to Coke Zero). The author has left it to me to bring the novice reader up to speed on the history of Sri Lanka and its glorious leader.

It would take a great historian and political commentator (such as Amarnath Amarasingam) to provide the ins-and-outs of the decades-long civil strife in Sri Lanka. Suffice it to say that in the early eighties, Tamil separatists ambushed a Sri Lankan army convoy. This incident and its backlash began the war. Led by their foul supreme commander Prabhakaran, the LTTE, or Tamil Tigers, held a succession of government administrations at bay, defeating their troops in the jungle and making fools of them around the negotiating table. It wasn't until my son came to power, aided by his brothers, that a decisive and victorious attack was mounted. The war came to an end and this elusive goal was finally realized in May, 2009.

There has been a lot of criticism from sour losers about the way Mahinda brought the war to an end, with the shelling of civilians and hospitals and the evacuation of aid workers and so on. To those I say: who actually wanted the war to continue one day longer? Did the means not justify the ends? Shouldn't my sons reward themselves for a job well done? There is nothing for a mother to be ashamed of here. Of course, there are some that say it's my fault for indulging them as young boys, that I should have strangled Mahinda at birth, or had a forced miscarriage. In fact, on my way over here, as my spirit flew through the air, I heard a film lecturer from the University of Peradeniya mutter to his friend: "If this motherfucker keeps eating the country, there'll be nothing left for us to stand on, save water." Is that any way for an intellectual and academic to speak? Yet, it is a mother's lot to put up with many such comments.

But enough about me. The one you're all interested in is, of course, my son Mahinda. Of all my boys, Mahinda was not the tallest or the strongest or the brightest or even the strangest (that title would go to Gota). Mahinda was not even the eldest. Chamal ranked him there. But he was the fiercest and the most wilful of his brothers. I daresay that if not for him, there would be no current Rajapaksa dynasty... forgive me, no *people's dynasty*. Things would have died out with his father, Don Alvin. May his soul find happiness wherever he is now, as long as it's not with me.

I know that many people will blame me for spawning this vicious lion of a man. When you're dead, you can't help but listen in on people's thoughts – it's a bit boring otherwise – if I had a rupee for every time some Sri Lankan opines and wishes I had had an abortion instead of giving birth to a monster, well, I'd have many lakhs of rupees... but I wouldn't know what to do with them. Everything in the afterlife is free.

Oh yes, Mahinda's birth! You will no doubt want to know something of the circumstances of his birth and his upbringing and childhood and so on. You'll want to know: did I do anything special that can be traced to his violent future and the twinning violent future of the country?

Mahinda might have been what we used to call a breech birth. He was prematurely big, weighing some five pounds near the beginning of the third trimester. Even then, he was restless and preferred to eat a lot. Sometimes, I admit, I'd have feverish dreams that he was gnawing on his umbilical cord with big teeth and then he'd go on to nibble up my intestines, would devour my heart, lungs, and spleen. He would consume the body that gave him life. I woke up with hot flashes and cold sweats. My husband would have to run out into the night, muttering curses, and fetch the doctor. Little foetus Mahinda seemed restless even then to get out into the world and conquer it. With all his movement in the womb, the doctor was worried that Mahinda would tangle himself up in the cord and produce severe complications. He suggested a C-section. I then realized the implications of the situation. With painful agony, I resolved that it was either going to be him or me. I put my foot down right then and there and with the doctor present, spread my legs. My petticoat fell between my wobbling knees and then I yelled down into my womb.

"Listen!" I cried, "I know you can hear me in there! You're *already* giving us trouble and you're not even born yet! Either you behave – be born like a normal boy – or your father is going to reach in there and spank your backside!"

I know Mahinda heard me because his legs stopped kicking. Very slowly, he untangled his feet from around the umbilical cord and the spasms stopped convulsing up my spine. My heart slowed down to a regular pace and I felt that my lungs and spleen might also be saved.

Things went smoothly after that and I gave birth the normal way at the end of the third trimester. However, the labour did take the better part of three days, as if Mahinda was trying to barrel out and the poor world, already knowing what it was in for, battled to keep him in.

The fortune teller dropped in on our little house in Hambantota the next day. We fed him tea and biscuits and he picked up little Mahinda. The fortune teller held the boy in his arms to search his face and divine his destiny. I am proud to say that Mahinda did not cry but abruptly grabbed the man's hand and tried to eat his fingers. The boy hadn't teethed yet but he bit so hungrily that the fortune teller cried in terror, dropped the child back into his cot, and ran out. He was so terrified that he didn't even stop to ask for payment.

"That's a first," said Don Alvin with wonderment. "A fortune teller that forgoes his fee? This boy is destined to make great changes and have influence over people!"

As a child, Mahinda didn't show much promise in school. Of course, years later, he would be awarded an honourary doctorate by the People's Friendship University of the Russian Federation for being a good friend and defeating terrorism. They really should change the name of that university. A musical ring, it does not have. The person sitting next to Mahinda at the convocation had earned his doctorate the slow way by studying for years and writing a dissertation on the economic prosperity of Asia. The only thing that sticks out about Mahinda's school years is that while the rest of the boys took electives like cricket and circuit analysis, Mahinda took home economics. He was the only boy in a class full of girls but did not seem perturbed by it. At first, we thought he had fallen in love with a girl in his class and this was his way of pursuing her but later surmised he simply wanted the leftovers from the dishes they cooked. We never did find out a definite answer.

It's tempting to think of Mahinda as a child whose appetite was so voracious that he devoured the country like a child in a Victorian nursery rhyme. I think this is a misguided idea. Mahinda's true genius lies a little closer to his father's operations as a land man. Being landowners, land has had particular significance to our family for generations. As a politician, Don Alvin was known for helping people of lower classes gain access to land and acquire deeds. Mahinda's eventual conquest of the Tamils was one of the most successful land distributions in this country's history. It was not a landowner's plot or a scheme but a successful redistribution of land in a way that was a little more unified, a little more stately. After all, the land belongs to no man: we belong to the land. We come out of it and we return to it. We live and die. So turns the dharma's wheel.

Many people have compared Mahinda to his nemesis, the hated and feared Velupillai Prabhakaran. I never met Prabhakaran, and have only glimpsed him in the afterlife, but there was something akin to a reflection between the two men. I know that my son felt conflicted emotions, both exultation and loss, on that fateful date in May when Prabhakaran's body was found. Both men were short, stocky, and some might even say rotund, gentlemen. They were ambitious and fearsome in their quiet ways. They sported moustaches and were gourmands. They came from rural backgrounds and perhaps, if they'd met under different circumstances, might have been friends. I don't know – Mahinda does keep his thoughts to himself but I suspect there are few he would consider worthy enough to be equal to Prabhakaran. Certainly, I knew my son envied Prabhakaran's moustaches, the vibrant and bristly way they adorned his face. Mahinda often compared his own hairy handlebar to that of Prabhakaran's. Apparently, Prabhakaran only wore his moustaches in times of war and shaved them during 'peace talks' (which were basically exercises in stalling and killing time, designed to make fools of the Singhalese). During talks, even before Mahinda came to power, my son would become sullen and angry around his wife and impatiently wait for Prabhakaran to regrow his moustache.

As for his wife, Shiranthi, I don't know what to say. My own mother would say that if you don't have something good to say, don't say anything at all. I will say that I would be lying if I were to claim I approved of their marriage. There's another saying we have in Hambantota: a woman must be like a good piece of land – firm, fertile, and able to put up with much fertilizer. My Mahinda might have been a little chubby and it's true, perhaps he did sweat quite a bit in his youth, but he could have done better for himself than a beauty queen and commodore's daughter! A commodore's daughter – seriously? Her knowledge might have been useful if we were under siege from pirates or didn't know which lipstick to apply before dinner. But what use could she be to a military genius who won his power in the boardrooms and battlefields of the nation?

Still, I can't abide the speculations and dark things trucked about in this book – we didn't discuss such things in my day. We were honest, but if Don Alvin read what these people write about, he would not have rested until all the people responsible for this book had their backsides properly caned. That's the way we raised our boys and that's the way that works. We have a third saying in Hambantota: spare the rod and you spoil the child, but of course they have this saying in other places too. We didn't know anything then about listening to children and being sensitive to their needs and so on. We didn't worry about it. All this modern rubbish. Where does it get you? A generation of ineffectual finger pointers and whiners. And before you point your fingers, which of you is innocent? Who is truly innocent these days? Perhaps a newborn baby during its first week of life is innocent... that's about it.

Anyway, you've gotten me off topic and my connection to the medium is growing weak. He must have eaten some buttery food for lunch because I feel it clogging up his arteries, making it hard to maintain my bond.

In any case, enough harsh words! To leaven the bitterness of these stories and to contribute my own little sweetness to their miserable world, I've decided to throw in my recipes for Mahinda's favourite dishes. Even if the situation is as dire as all these petitioners claim, here are some Sri Lankan dishes you can prepare in the comfort of your own home to make these stories more palatable. As my illustrious son says, there's very little that's so bad in the world that it cannot be remedied by a morsel or two of tasty food!

Now, this has been a pleasure but I must get going. Enjoy the recipes and if you see Don Alvin, don't tell him that you saw me....

Butter Cake

This recipe, like all the recipes in this book, will serve four people. Unless you're cooking for someone like my son, Mahinda. Then, it might make two servings – if you're lucky! In that case, simply send the servant out for double the ingredients and if the servant curses or mutters imprecations under his breath, simply remind him of who's paying the wages.

Ingredients:
½ lbs butter
½ lbs sugar
4 eggs
½ lbs white flour
2 teaspoons baking powder
1 teaspoon vanilla extract
¼ cup milk

First, beat the butter and sugar together until you achieve a consistent mixture. I usually got Don Alvin to do this part as he was so skilled in the art of beating. Then I would get him to beat in the eggs. Meanwhile, I would mix the flour and baking powder together and then sift the mixture using a fine mesh. Have you done that? Good. Now, gently mix the flour and baking powder with the egg batter. Then, add the vanilla and milk to the mix.

The entire thing should be baked in a preheated oven at 325 Fahrenheit for 35 mins. You can test it by poking it with a knife. Just have fun with it and pretend you're the coroner at the 'Lessons Learnt and Reconciliation

Commission.' If the knife pulls out cleanly, the cake is ready (and the victim is dead!)

When done, take it out of the oven and let it rest for 10 mins. before eating with friends when they arrive for tea.

Tamil Nightmares

The dream always begins with four dark ladies.

The ladies had less than half their lives before them. They knew this and the only thing that could offset the sweet misery of their slow departure from youth was the authority and certitude that came with it. They knew, for example, which one of their nieces was throwing her career away pursuing a degree in the social sciences, which man was no good as a husband, and which grandchild would rescue the faltering family reputation and whom all hopes must be pinned upon. Sarojini aunty, Lakshmi aunty, Deepa aunty, and Rekha aunty had been meeting at each other's houses in the afternoon since they were children. As girls in Jaffna, they would get together after school, growing comfortable in each other's company, trading dolls for gossip. After they arrived in England, one by one, they came together as often as their busy lives and families would permit, their girlish giggles now supplanted by hoarse cackles and throaty guffaws. Their ribbons and makeup had long been replaced by thick jewellery and chains of gossip and opinion which wove a stiff ring around their lives. The flighty awkwardness of their immigrant lives had thickened into a limey comfort and tyrannical stubbornness. They ruled over their families like vultures, not stirring from their roost. Over time, their eyes became clearer, their beaks sharper.

Sarojini's nephew had now married a Singhalese girl and as the leader of their stubborn group, she commanded the most sympathy. For years, the other women had allowed her to air her grievances first, doling out tea for sympathy. Lakshmi's daughter was moving from undergrad to grad school with no clear direction, muddled as ever. Deepa and Rekha were both grandmothers, having married their children off young, and revelled in the daily complaint of how tiresome their grandchildren were, how they lived now only to serve them.

They were at Sarojini's house and she seated them, fussing after them to such an extent that they could never have cause to complain. She served them deluxe crackers with lemon filling and large granules of sugar sprinkled on top, tea with cardamom, and liberal slices of butter cake. They encouraged her to stop fussing, to sit down; as the host, she was entitled to the spotlight, the primary wave of attention.

Lakshmi aunty patted the seat on the sofa beside her, "Sarojini, stop it and sit down! Tell us all about your nephew. What's he doing now?"

Sarojini aunty sat down, the sofa cushion sinking beneath her weight, a small porcelain saucer of tea held daintily in her hand. She raised the cup and blew on the tea, took a tentative sip, and wrinkled her face. "What is there to say? What can I say that hasn't been said before?"

"We tell them, again and again, until our voices go dry," said Deepa aunty patiently.

Taking the cue, Sarojini aunty put her cup down and jumped in, waving her hands, "Do you know what that boy is doing now? He's taken out a loan and his wife, who as you all know thinks of nothing but money, wants them to start a hamburger restaurant. A hamburger restaurant, can you believe it? 'We don't even eat meat,' I told him. 'You're supposed to be Hindu. What do you know about hamburgers?'

"'I know about making money,' he said. 'We're not going to eat it. We're going to sell it,' added his wife.

She's made him like her so fast, I can't believe it! And you know what the worst is? They expect to serve to Hindu children. They're expecting the boys to come in and defile themselves. He even wants to give it a Hindu name: *Durga Burger*."

The other ladies gasped.

"He wants a large sign of the Goddess in the front window, each of her six hands holding a burger, French fries, onion rings, a milkshake, an apple pie, and a chicken wing!"

"Do they have no shame?" asked Lakshmi aunty. "Where will we all end up?"

"I'm not worried," replied Sarojini aunty with a stoic wave of her hand. Her bangles clattered as she picked up her teacup and drank. The story timed perfectly, the milky brew was just the right temperature now. She placed the teacup back on its saucer with deep satisfaction. "If I know that boy, he'll run this into the ground like everything else. And then come crying to me. And I'll tell him I told you so."

"Don't give him any more money. You must draw a line," declared Rekha aunty authoritatively.

"But then his wife will push him to try something else," muttered Deepa aunty, looking down with austerity at her long wrinkled fingers.

"He'll want to cater to the Portuguese Tamil community."

"And call it *Burgher Burger!*"

They all shrieked with laughter.

"Those Singhalese will do anything," continued Deepa aunty darkly, staring into the black dregs of her teacup.

"Did I ever tell you about the time in the early eighties when my husband, may he rest in peace, was a lawyer in the Colombo high courts? If he lived to see how things have turned out today, he would shoot himself and fall back into his grave."

The other ladies had heard many stories about Deepa's husband, with his towering frame and magisterial voice, who had interrogated defendants so intimidatingly that they had suffered heart attacks. The old barrister had been kidnapped and was never heard from again, but was alive more than ever in the reminiscences of his mournful wife.

"Mahinda Rajapaksa was a lawyer in those days. He was a failed politician and a hanger-on in the judicial scene in Colombo. This was before he made enemies for trying to get the United Nations interested in the JVP killings. The irony of how things have changed!

"In any case, some friends of my husband who held him in high esteem threw a birthday party for our first girl. She was only seven then. They were eager to curry favour from my husband and spared no expense. They made reservations at the Galle Face Hotel and you should have seen how the food flowed! The tablecloths and the service! The napkins even. Everything the very best! Somehow, Rajapaksa had been invited or had wrangled an invitation; many of my husband's colleagues were prominent Singhalese lawyers and politicians.

"So, he arrived late to the party, without any children of his own. He was in a grey sharkskin suit and clutched a briefcase. This was before he wore that traditional white kurta and shawl, his costume for politics. He had a very thick orange tie and he was sweating constantly around his fat neck. He seemed uncomfortable and agitated and kept on pulling at his big moustache; he looked like a villain from a James Bond movie. Frankly, I was afraid he would scare the children.

"The children had finished their games and the cake had been cut and eaten; all the presents had been opened. So he arrives and slams his briefcase down on a table and pulls out a wad of something wrapped in pink paper. Only, it seemed like the paper had been wrapped so hurriedly and messily I wondered whether it was a package of fish he was carrying. I pushed our daughter to be polite and go accept the gift.

"She took it from him and even at that age, she seemed hesitant to take the gift from the strange, uncomfortable man. Inside was a G. I. Joe doll in a box. It was a white doll of a blond-haired man with combat fatigues and a rocket launcher. We looked at this box in surprise and then my daughter said 'look, Amma, what's this say?' A small envelope with a card had dropped out of the back. I picked up the envelope and opened it. The writing was in English. Now, my English wasn't perfect so I had to read it slowly, and it took me twice as long to understand what was going on. When I understood, my blood went through the roof. My husband was the intimidating one, but I could have killed that cheap bastard right there! This nobody, this nothing, who hadn't even been invited, had re-wrapped a gift someone else had given him and brought it to my daughter's birthday. It must have been given to him in America by someone who thought he had sons. He hadn't even taken the time to find the envelope and card and remove them!"

The women chuckled ruefully. "What did you do?" asked Lakshmi aunty after she had stopped laughing.

"What could we do? We got the hotel to get him some food and fed him. Everyone avoided him and after half an hour, he left without telling anybody."

"You think that's bad?" put in Rekha aunty. "Well, sit back and I'll tell you all something that'll make the hair on your arms curl."

Deepa aunty, her need for sympathy soothed, now sat back and graciously gave the spotlight to Rekha. As dramatic as Rekha's teaser had been, it was universally acknowledged that they should all get up to refill their teacups. Lemon biscuits were liberally passed around. Saris were straightened and blouses readjusted.

"Well," said Rekha aunty, "this isn't something that I've ever told any of you before. To tell the truth, it's not something I want people to know. But we're close, aren't we? I know that you'll understand and feel my misery, the sorrow I've been carrying around for more than twenty years. I don't know why I haven't told you before."

"Stop being nervous," said Sarojini aunty, "you're among friends here." The others murmured and sipped their teas. Lakshmi aunty burped, due to her bad stomach.

"Well, as I said, it was some time ago. Just after the '77 riots. I had a niece – the eldest daughter of my eldest sister – she lives in Portland now. She went to the States for the first time to meet her husband and get married. She's a nurse there still – you've seen photos of her and her family. When she moved out there, she was very young and I went there along with her mother and another one of our friends to help her. We escorted her to the wedding hall stage and before that, washed her, dressed her, reassured her. She was so nervous and continually asked us for advice. One of the things she asked me was what good deed she should do on the day of her wedding. As you know, the bride is supposed to do a good deed, something substantial, to bring her good luck, good karma, in her ensuing marriage and in her life.

"I told her – remember, this was just after the '77 riots where they'd burned those houses and killed those Tamils because the TULF had gotten so many votes – that she should adopt a Sri Lankan child through World Vision. She wasn't going to adopt the child and have her live with her, you understand. She was moving to the States. She would adopt an orphan in Sri Lanka and send some money every month through World Vision. So she took my advice and signed up to adopt a child and got on with her wedding.

"We naturally assumed that the child would be Tamil – a lot of Tamils had just been killed or displaced because of the riots and I'm sure she told World Vision that she was Tamil and that's why she was sponsoring an orphan. Well, World Vision wouldn't allow my niece to pick and choose – she didn't have power over whether the child was Tamil. She wrote a Tamil letter in good faith to her new ward from her home in the States. To her shock, when they sent her a folder with a photo and description of the child, there was no return letter. The child was Singhalese! She had committed to supporting a Singhalese child for the rest of his natural childhood. Well, as you might guess, she didn't speak Singhalese and he didn't speak Tamil. So, just as she was learning to live in America and starting to work on her English, she had to write letters in English to this child that she didn't want. But she didn't dare cancel her sponsorship."

"How could she?" asked Lakshmi aunty. "Think about the repercussions to her marriage!"

"Exactly," continued Rekha, "the marriage, the repercussions. So my niece didn't say anything to her new husband or her family. She just told me as I had given her the idea. I felt badly for her because I was somewhat responsible so I said 'What can you do? He's a child. He doesn't know anything. You must keep writing.'

"So she bit her lip and continued sending her monthly letter as best she could. The two tried to continue writing to each other even though both of them had the English of seven-year-olds. The letters started to dwindle and eventually, both stopped writing to each other and my niece just continued sending money. She sent extra on Vesak and other Buddhist holidays as if she herself was Buddhist. She took the money out of her own personal allowance and kept it up religiously until the boy turned eighteen, never missing a payment. It was as if she had a contract with the Devil himself.

"She said that the day he turned eighteen was the best day of her life. She went out on a drive just to be alone and screamed where no one could hear her."

"How horrible," murmured the others.

"I haven't told the worst of it yet," sighed Rekha, her chest heaving slowly, her words slowing down. "My niece lost touch with the child but she heard that he didn't graduate from school. She heard from his foster parents that he had a very unhappy and troubled life. He joined the Sri Lankan Army and left them. The last they heard, he was involved in the fighting over Elephant Pass around 1997. He deserted the army and was supposedly involved in a massacre of Tamils in a village outside of Kilinochchi. My niece never heard from him again. But she has nightmares once in a while that he shows up at her doorstep in America, holding a machete with blood on his hands...."

"You're lucky to at least have a niece and children that are all grown up and well-taken care of," sighed Lakshmi aunty. "All of you – *my* daughter is still in school. 'What's the point of all this school if you don't know what you're doing?' I ask her. This is the worst time it's ever been to raise children. None of them care about values anymore, about being good. They've all become corrupted by life here. My daughter's going to school in London as you know, and running around who knows where? When I call her at night, she doesn't answer the phone."

The rest of the women sighed, imagining the worst, causing Lakshmi aunty to burp again.

"I'm going to get a call from the police one of these days, asking me to come identify her body in a gutter. What's the point of leaving things back home if these young people just forget everything and destroy themselves? At least it's better to stay home and be killed there, where they can die for a cause and you can go to your child's funeral with some dignity."

"What's she doing in school now?" asked Rekha.

"She's just graduated from her undergrad degree in Postcolonial Literature and is moving on to her M.Phil. What is the point of all this reading if it doesn't make you smart?"

"At least she's educated – it will make her a better match."

"If anyone will want her," snorted Lakshmi aunty, "she takes this too far and no one will be interested. Just you wait and see! You know, I went to visit her once, without telling her?

"I went to her address in the evening, a communal house in Soho. She wasn't even home. What does she do there? All these people and tourists coming and going. How is she affording to live there? I'm her mother and I don't know anything.

"As I was leaving, there was a crazy person shouting on the street corner. The only thing was that he wasn't shouting in a crazy way that you or I might understand. He wasn't shouting about Jesus or that we needed to be saved. He was shouting about Jane Austen. *Jane Austen!* Can you believe it?

"He stood on a box and yelled out: 'Jane Austen died for your sins! Jane Austen lived alone and never married and devoted herself to writing so that you could benefit. Stop and realize that Jane Austen died for your sins!' I said, 'Come down off there and get yourself something to eat.' I tried to give him money but he only glared at me. Perhaps he knows my daughter? It was all very strange. Even the crazy people are different in her world. What will I do?"

*

Mahinda Rajapaksa woke up in his London hotel room drenched in sweat. The top of his kurta was soaked thoroughly and the sweat had gotten into the bedclothes and felt damp and heavy underneath his back. He remembered slowly where he was. Why this dream now? It came back again and again. The stories were different but the women were always the same. He understood Tamil and knew what they said. Were they reminiscent of women he had known as a child?

He got up slowly and looked at the alarm clock. It was 5:42 p.m. Picking up his earth-coloured shawl, he draped it around his shoulders protectively and walked over to the curtains. Peering through the window, he could see the

English Tamil mob shaking their fists and stamping their feet and rattling their placards, chanting threats into the hazy air. He was so high up in the hotel that he could not hear them but he could see each individual head, curly with black hair, looking up at him, could form ghostly Tamil syllables in the rising air from their vociferous throats. There would be no address; the speech was cancelled, so there was no reason for him to hurry or stir.

Beat your breasts, ladies, he thought to himself, *now is the time to beat your breasts and wail! What else can you do?*

Milk Toffee

I must have told Mahinda a thousand times, when I was alive, to drink plenty of milk as a way to ward off sweat during nightmares. But would that boy listen? Why would he listen to me? After all, I'm only his mother. I only carried him in my womb for a torturous nine months and seven days.

In any case, who can stay mad at Mahinda for long? He has such a plucky agreeable face! To treat him, I would make one of his favourite sweets – milk toffee!

Ingredients:
1 can of condensed milk
½ lbs sugar
1 teacup water
¼ teaspoon of cardamom
1 teaspoon of vanilla extract
¼ cup of crushed white cashews
1 tablespoon of butter

Grab a pan and mix the sugar, water, and condensed milk into it. Cook the concoction over low heat, making sure to constantly stir. When it becomes golden brown, add in the cashews, vanilla, cardamom, and butter. As soon (and I mean immediately!) as the mixture thickens, pour it into a greased pan. Try to refrain from pulling it apart and eating from the pan. We are *not* animals! Cut the mixture into one-inch squares as soon as you can and allow them to cool.

The Last Tiger in Sri Lanka

The reports came in from the region surrounding the Sigiriya rock fortress that a tiger had been seen terrorizing villagers. It was large and silent as it strode through the glades at night, swallowing Singhalese and Tamil children indiscriminately. It even ate people's leftover curries and did not bother to clear away the mess of the broken pottery shards or plantain leaves.

Sri Lanka was known for its leopards and its devil birds. Christopher Ondaatje has said much about the devil bird's haunting, soul-piercing cry so there's no reason to dwell upon it, but no one had ever spotted an actual tiger before. In fact, rumours began to abound that this was one of the tiger cubs purported to be owned by Prabhakaran as a youth, and that it had somehow gotten loose and avoided capture. If so, it must be very old. Of course, the other tigers that had existed in the country were not tigers precisely but LTTE, the Liberation Tigers of Tamil Eelam, a ragtag cult of terrorist youths and grumpy children, forced to serve their plump and pudding-faced supreme commander, Velupillai Prabhakaran.

Rajapaksa and his brothers, especially the ruthless Gota, put paid to them. It had been more than three years since the end of the decades-long civil war. Three Victory Day parades had come and gone and Rajapaksa was victorious! Whatever Tigers had once existed had fled, were rehabilitated, or had been killed. Rajapaksa had delivered on his electoral promises. Despite the absolute success of his enterprise and the wealth that flowed into the coffers of the Rajapaksa dynasty, the flutter of peace and the intensity of joy that should see him, by all rights, crowned emperor, eluded him. Few people knew that this was not an outcome he had initially sought. As a young man, during the early sixties, he had not wanted to be a politician at all like his father and his uncle, but an amazing actor. The greatest actor the country had ever seen!

He wished to be the crowning jewel of Singhalese cinema! The Singhalese Sean Connery. The Sri Lankan sex machine. Yet none of it had passed. Not even the sex machine part. Instead, he had become the lead in a movie called *Sri Lanka Part IV: A New Hope!* He was the star in a shimmering epoch rivalling any in Sri Lanka's history. He was a modern king! An emperor!

And yet, he was not respected. He knew this. He was feared but not respected. He was obeyed but not loved. Taking an inspirational leaf from Her Highness, Queen Elizabeth the Second, Rajapaksa had ordered the Sri Lankan treasury to issue a thousand-rupee note featuring his likeness. Unfortunately, soon after these notes were issued into circulation, strange reports were heard. Some of the notes quickly became soggy with spittle and phlegm. Many were defaced. Others had clearly been used to scrub the toilets. Merchants refused to take them and the banks had to accept them back (with tweezers) on a daily basis and have them destroyed.

But now there was a tiger. A real Bengal tiger, *panthera tigris tigris,* was seen slumping around villagers' huts, sticking its head into the pots of the previous night's cooking, messing up the gardens of middle-class homeowners. Troubled sightings reported the beast at three metres long. Reports further identified the tiger as mostly vegetarian, except for the times it ate people. No one could tell what its proclivities might be on any given night. It devoured some children and spared others. It ate some meat dishes and avoided others. It especially had a thing for rice and ghee and curds, making it a bit of a gourmand amongst its brethren. However, it was not above devouring the occasional pot of goat curry and when the Ondaatje family's prize-winning labradoodle Lucky disappeared, leaving nothing but a prize-winning heap of small bones and delicate fur, it was decided that something should be done. *Something should be done?* thought Rajapaksa. *What? Was there no hero to step up and do something about this very dire situation?* Waiting for animal control from the Yala National Park meant that the surrounding villagers might as well just give up! Rajapaksa stepped up.

It was a clarion call to arms from life and the warrior's blood once again boiled in Rajapaksa's veins. This was the moment he had been waiting for. He actually owned a vast collection of tiger hunting memorabilia and weaponry from the time of the British Raj. As a boy, he had a special interest in the Sepoy Mutiny. He pulled out the scarlet-red colonial sergeant's coat that had once belonged to a member of the 40th regiment, long since disbanded. The coat sat in a dusty display case and he had to pull it over his broad arms and shoulders; the seams ripped and the buttons flew off but he got it on – the man who had worn it before had been slight and spindly. Rajapaksa's legs were stuffed into a pair of starched, stainless breeches with even greater difficulty. The tight trousers almost completely cut off his circulation, turning the flesh around his privates blue and giving him varicose veins, but he managed to walk forward, bowlegged, and grab the pith helmet that soon completed the outfit. Stroking his moustaches, Rajapaksa picked a vintage twelve-bore elephant gun from his collection. With mounting excitement, he fished out black powder cartridges which were then stuffed into his cartridge satchel. Now, all he needed was an elephant to carry him into battle so that he could have an advantage over the beast when they inevitably met.

Catching an elephant wasn't easy. For one thing, he couldn't do it alone and several soldiers had to accompany him to a path near the Pinnawala Elephant Orphanage. Elephants which had been maimed or harmed during the civil war lived here in sanctuary. What Rajapaksa was doing was strictly illegal, but he had heard tales of how in the old days, elephants were trapped and bidden not with force, but with bribery and amenable civility. The mahouts would stake out a clearing where elephants were to pass and then leave nooses of deer hide lying on the ground. The other ends of the nooses were attached to nearby trees. Rajapaksa and his posse did this.

They had to be patient and wait in stillness for hours.

Their dedication was eventually rewarded when a lone elephant recklessly placed its front leg into one of the nooses. At a signal from Rajapaksa, one of the soldiers ran up and tightened the noose so that the elephant's leg was caught. The elephant immediately reared its giant head and trunk, stomping and struggling with a force greater than a battle tank, ready to cut down trees with its fury. The boys dodged and manoeuvred and though there was a tradition of doing things this way, more than one felt he would meet his end that day, that it was not worth the SLA paycheque. The elephant made a terrific racket, crashing down the trees on either side of the road. It flattened the ground so that the echoes of its stomping reverberated up the soldiers' boots and they felt their eyes slammed to the top of their skulls. However, over the course of the following hour, two more legs were caught and tightened in nooses so that the poor elephant's legs were splayed apart and its fury pulled in three cardinal directions.

Rajapaksa noted then that the elephant had had his remaining foot blown off by a mine and that all the poor creature had left was a flailing tapered stump. This last tentacle, like a second trunk, snaked and slithered on the ground with a venomous resistance as if it seethed and contained the elephant's concentrated rancour, his feeling and reaction at this ignominious predicament.

This leg, too, was caught and tied awkwardly. Rajapaksa spent the next few hours feeding the elephant sweets and crackers and even some of his own mother's special milk toffee that he had gotten the cooks to prepare. He didn't mind bribing the elephant to win it over but having to be patient and calm the elephant, tame him, made Rajapaksa nervous. He was used to his wishes being fulfilled in short order and it was often through kickbacks, greased palms, and promises of favours that he achieved this perfect state of calm and bliss. As he fed the elephant toffee after toffee, cracker after cracker, he kept one in ten crackers and toffees (or one tenth of the government state contract) back for himself. He knew that his brother Basil would expect this as standard procedure.

Rajapaksa thought about Basil and the other boys as the party set out the following day to track the tiger. They had come back to Sri Lanka from the States after Rajapaksa's bid for leadership. Even Gota who had sworn to never see his older brother if he could help it (there was too much blood under that bridge) had eventually reneged and returned to take up the Secretary of Defense position. Only Dudley remained, somewhat aloof, somewhat distant, in America.

The procession set forth on the trunk road from Kandy to Sigiriya. Rajapaksa's entourage included government ministers, soldiers, tentage and furniture, grand table fare, a shikari (experienced game hunter), and a mahout for Rajapaksa's elephant. His brothers were noticeably missing from the party because they secretly thought Rajapaksa's quest to kill the tiger a fool's errand. Besides, thought Rajapaksa as he continually plied the elephant with sweets and crackers, the success of his mission would be that much sweeter if he alone accomplished it. The howdah atop the elephant was crowded with items from Col. Rajapaksa's colonial arms collection: various handguns, Hindoo thug daggers, and his prized 12-bore, double-barrelled rifle, manufactured by W & J Kavanagh, Dublin, in the 1800s.

Last night, he had almost not been able to sleep, what with the feverish anticipation and excitement he felt for today's hunt and all. He would have been happier riding a magnificent lion than an elephant – that was to be sure. Elephants were so slow when not stampeding and unlike horses, were not demure or compliant. Plus, this one limped! One could not spur and control an elephant in the traditional sense, the mahout had told him – they must be reasoned with and enticed to cooperate. The glory of his Singhalese race traced its ancestry back to Prince Vijaya who brought the lion banner from India across the Palk Strait and into Sri Lanka. King Dutugemunu had also carried it proudly in battle against the Hindu king Elara. His own uncle, D. M. Rajapaksa, was called the Lion of Ruhuna and bore the proud claim of being the first in their family to take political office. Rajapaksa had never been too close to his own father, D. A., and took inspiration from his uncle D. M. instead. Rajapaksa even wore a shawl that was the same kurakkan colour as his uncle's.

The problem was that there were no actual lions in Sri Lanka. There never had been. It was a borrowed symbol, an invention, a fantasy that had somehow wormed in and perpetuated through the ages; the symbol dug its claws into the carcass of the country's imagination and would not release its hold. Of course, there were no tigers either. Until now.

The mystery tantalized. Rajapaksa had finally fallen asleep in the lean hours of the morning earlier that day. The large frame of his wife turned in fits and starts, snoring like an air raid siren. In spite of this, he dreamt that he was a large tawny lion, stretching his claws, and running through the breadth and length of the land from Adam's Peak to the Palk Strait. His mane flowed behind him and a large rumbling roar came from within his chest, announcing might and virility into the hot night.

In his dream, he came through the undergrowth to the foot of the Sigiriya fortress which glowed yellow like a cat's eyes in the night. He was a lion and it was ancient times for the Lion's Head entrance to the fortress no longer lay in ruins. It reared its mighty stone head above its giant paws in communion with him. Its protracted claws heralded him in rock-like recognition. The breeze shifted, the grasses rustled, and mighty Rajapaksa could smell something foreign, waiting for him beyond the entrance. On the stone steps leading up into the mouth of the fortress... it was another cat but not like him. It was longer, hunched haunches, a terrible coiled spring of a tail. Midnight stripes underneath the moon.

A tiger!

It moved silently, refused to roar. Rajapaksa could feel the cold and menace emanating from its mandibles. Rajapaksa circled around, climbed the rock using great strenuous handholds, passed the mirror wall where he could see his glorious mane and porcelain green eyes reflected in the warm moonlight. He approached the tiger from behind. He sprang on the animal and flattened it to the steps where it crouched behind a boulder, sinking his razor-sharp claws into the tiger's shoulders and flanks. The tiger struggled but Rajapaksa crushed him with his weight, with his force, with his very will. He broke the tiger's ribs and gouged the flesh around his eyes, blinding him. And then, when the tiger was finally dazed, unconscious, and broken, Rajapaksa swatted aside the tiger's frazzled, shredded tail. He lifted up its battered haunches, and thrust his own engorged, tumescent lion's shaft into the soft tissues of the tiger's anus. Again and again went the shaft, willing the tiger into submission.

Rajapaksa had woken with adrenalin shooting through his veins and panic clutching his throat. He had not been able to get back to sleep and the dream and its attendant mania seemed to linger even now, hours later, as they approached the rock fortress. His legs seemed to kick with no act or will of their own. The sun was starting to descend in the sky. The rock, orange streaked with chalky brown, glowed like a priest's robe. In the distance, he could see the decapitated lumbering body of the animal clothed in rock. What did the dream mean? Would it not mean that he would be victorious against the tiger today, just as he had been victorious against the Liberation Tigers three and a half years ago?

They passed the giant standing Buddha statue near the foot of the rock and the party was forced to stop and pay obeisance and involve themselves in prayer. Rajapaksa marvelled at the stylized white folds of cloth that clung to the standing Buddha with dark hair and gold ornamentation. What a romancing of the stone!

He remembered the time long ago when he and his brothers had come here as children.

Their father, D. A. Rajapaksa, initially MP for Beliatta, had been granted the position of Cabinet Minister of Agriculture and Lands in the mid-fifties after he had followed Bandaranaike and crossed the floor to change parties. D. A. had initially become known for initiating schemes to transfer land holdings to homeless peasants and in his new position as Minister of Agriculture and Lands, he had to travel to Sigiriya to talk to some of the Buddhist monks that ran things around there. He took the boys along on a day trip. While D. A. was busy talking to the head monks, he left the boys to explore the rock fortress.

"Don't get into any trouble," warned their father, "or I'll tan your backsides!"

Even then, Mahinda had been the de facto leader of the rest of the boys. Chamal was older and Mahinda deferred to him for formality's sake when family was around but it was understood that Chamal was too reserved, too ineffectual, to have much impact as a leader. That duty fell to Mahinda. He sometimes conferred with Chamal for his superior knowledge and in this way, the peace was kept. Mahinda was always conscious of pleasing their father who could fly into a terrible temper at times, especially when his parliamentary duties pressed – in those times, D. A. would beat everybody in the house simply to be fair and leave no opportunity for discipline wasted.

Left to themselves, the boys' personalities came out. Basil was always off on his own, as easily fascinated by a line of ants trailing across the rock or burning them with a magnifying glass to watch them scatter. Gota was difficult and unpredictable even then, at turns angry and boisterous. He was too hotheaded and it fell to Mahinda to try and calm the boy down, to use force if necessary. That only left Dudley, sweet Dudley. Dudley was the youngest of the boys and their father's favourite. Anyone who met Dudley understood why. Dudley seemed to make up for whatever was missing or objectionable in the other boys' personalities. With his angelic face and beatific demeanour, the boy could win over even the fiercest of bullies, could temper the roughest of hearts.

At first, at the fortress, the boys had played explorers and then this had soon changed to a game of playing Prince Vijaya and his followers, discovering Sri Lanka for the first time. Rajapaksa was Vijaya, of course. Only Gota was rankled and upset by this obvious choice. Rajapaksa appeased him by promising to let the younger boy have a turn in the role of Prince Vijaya, knowing that Gota would soon forget and become distracted by something else.

The boys became tired and hot after nearly an hour of playing their explorer games. Prince Vijaya had finally landed with his ferocious clan near Adam's Peak, within Ruhuna, and named the land 'Tambapanni.' What was to be done now? The sun was sinking but the heat still seared their heads; the tourists had dwindled down and the boys were left to themselves. They walked around in search of shady cloisters. So doing, they came in sight of the frescoes of women floating near the bottom of the rock face. The large women's breasts were ripe, exposed, and pointed with nubile potency. The colours, their golden bellies, their sharp eyes, and the perfumed green plants in their hair made the boys stop and collectively gasp. Gota, Mahinda, Chamal, and Basil all began to clutch the bulges that were pressing against their pants and making them sweat anew, uncomfortably shifting from one foot to the other. Where was their father and what was taking him so long?

Listing as it limped, the elephant made slow progress, and the tiger party came within a hundred metres of the great rock fort and camped for the evening. Rajapaksa rewarded the elephant by not taking his own customary ten percent of the toffees and crackers, allowing the poor beast to have them all. Everybody sat down, set up tents, pulled out tables and laid them with food, set up portable DVD players so that the guests could watch videos of the last Victory Day parade and various speeches Rajapaksa had made. At night, they heard the devil bird call out his ominous cry and wondered about the legend that claimed death was imminent for the hearer. Rajapaksa felt a slight shiver pass through his body. He hoped that the tiger, who must be around, heard it also and that the call was meant for the striped beast and not himself. They could almost sense the great jungle cat, grown ten times larger than life, stalking about in the night, living in the leaping flames of their fire. Someone invoked the first stanza of Blake's famous poem and they all listened in mesmerized fear:

> *Tyger! Tyger! burning bright*
> *in the forests of the night*
> *What fearful hand or eye*
> *could frame thy fearful symmetry?*

Rajapaksa ordered the company all to sleep and they packed away the tables, the cloths, the utensils, the portable DVD players, and the rest of it. They then retired to fitful handfuls of sleep. The elephant had already found a cool grove some way off and for a while, its sweet rumbling snores were the only things that could be heard in the still air.

That night, Rajapaksa fell into a deep sleep, exhausted. He dreamt of them then, the five boys at Sigiriya before the dark thing that happened. Rajapaksa could not say exactly what that dark thing was but the boys did not talk of it afterwards and it hung between them like some dread noose placed around their necks, a deep compact that held them together yet pushed them far apart, then and permanently.

The boys had been exhausted and sought shade near the mirror wall, a face of smooth porcelain stone where rulers had once been able to look at their reflections. History had it that the king, who had set up the fortress, paranoid and mad for power, had killed his own father by walling him in a chamber while the old man was still alive. A suffocating, lightless death.

On what remained of the mirror wall, poets and passersby had written slogans and lines of verse. They expressed beauty or reverence or just plain aimlessness: *I am Budal. Came with all my family to see Sigiriya*, began one such inscription. Gota pulled out a marker and in his immature eight-year-old way, began to write profanities on the wall. He adorned his profanities with drawings of stick figures in all sorts of filthy sexual congress, perhaps inspired by the visions of floating women on the rock face below. Where had the boy become so adept in filth, what manner of idiocy would he carry out next? This was answered when one of the things he wrote was *Mahinda is a Big Asshole!* Rajapaksa, as the leader of their party, was about to clout him when Basil took the pen from Gota and gleefully drew a huge hairy cock and balls. Chamal then took the pen and, giggling despite himself, drew a hand giving the rude 'V' sign and then wrote *Bollocks!* in huge letters beneath it. This was their modern response to the fifteen-hundred pieces of ancient writing before them, to the beautiful frescoes of the bathing women.

A foul-tempered priest who chanced by did not see things their way. This man was stringy and strict. He caught them drawing profanities on the ancient and holy wall. Though he was definitely growing out of adolescence and a near adult, Chamal suddenly found his ear being caught and twisted by the priest's vice-like grip. Not letting go, the priest with his wiry golden frame, severe features, and striking black mane of hair, adjusted his robe with his other hand, pulling the folds tightly around his waist. "Now, what's going on here?" he roared.

The boys stammered and protested but the priest cut down their cries with a cat-like glare. The boys did not even have enough time to explain that they were sons of a minister and dignitary. "Somebody's going to have to pay," said the priest and looked around. Rajapaksa was old enough to realize what was happening: they were being squeezed – he had seen his father work his way through similar situations a couple of times – but none of the boys had any money.

"We're very sorry, sir, we'll wash it off immediately," came a small voice. Everybody turned to look at Dudley, sweet Dudley, smaller than the rest of them, venturing forward to bow down before the priest. Dudley offered him a humble smile. So sweet and pure, so religious at such a young age, the youngest Rajapaksa must have been horrified at what his older brothers had done. Dudley had not partaken, had felt too junior to reprimand, but now he spoke up, hoping to make things right.

"What was that?" asked the priest, shocked at the young boy's boldness.

"We are very sorry, sir. May you and the Buddha forgive us. My brothers did not mean it and our father would kill us if he found out. Please don't tell him. Please let us wash it off."

"Your father would kill you..." the priest looked down at that sweet angelic face, its dimpled cheeks and clear bright eyes, the softly parted lips that belied a hurt expression full of tenderness and warmth. The priest's leonine expression seemed to swallow the young boy in its maw. "Of course, of course," whispered the priest, as if thinking to himself, and let go Chamal's ear. Chamal winced and adjusted his glasses, surreptitiously gave the marker back to Gota.

"Well, I suppose..." mused the priest, re-tucking the folds of his robe, "one of you will have to come get the water and the soap."

"I'll get it," volunteered Rajapaksa, sighing.

"Not you. The little one." The priest forcefully jutted his chin at Dudley.

The other boys looked at each other, not knowing what was happening. A sharpness like a cat's swipe twisted their guts. The boys looked at the mirror wall, then looked up at each other. Dudley still seemed wounded, or scared and swallowed up.

Slowly, the boys nodded at each other, then turned to Mahinda and Chamal, not saying anything. The two elder boys met each other's eyes uncertainly. There was confusion and fear, but why? Whether that confusion rested upon the prospect of their father suddenly returning and then beating them all or something else was uncertain.... A strange understanding without words hung between the boys. The priest sensed their answer.

"Right, then – " the priest muttered disaffectedly and once more tucked his robe in at the waist. His tension dismounting, his shoulders relaxed, the man looked back at Dudley and for the first time, eased his lips into a smile. Shaking his mane, the priest placed a hand on Dudley's shoulder and led him up the steep steps.

The boys waited. And waited. And waited. Finally, Dudley returned, carrying a pail with some water in it and a sponge. The water had already gone lukewarm and the soap had flattened into a greasy sworl. Dudley's shirt was untucked and his hair was dishevelled. A small cut had turned into a welt upon his right cheek. Had the boy been cut prior to their climb? Rajapaksa could not remember.

Dudley said nothing but simply sat there and crouched, staring in the distance, while the other boys scrubbed and scrubbed at the profane graffiti they had added to the wall's surface. It was as if they were not simply scrubbing pen lines but at a wire trap that had been drawn around them, unable to dent the hair-thin weave. They endeavoured to scrub the disgust of the day from their nostrils.

*

The next morning, the men in the hunting party woke as the sun threw forth glowing waves of undulating orange light across the land and rock. They seemed to file into the melting land itself as they paraded past the large fortress. Rajapaksa looked up with a telescope at the mirror wall from his perch atop the elephant and again saw the same graffiti he had seen many years ago: *Mahinda is a big asshole!* Was this a coincidence? Did someone else now know about that day? Or was it another Mahinda that the words referred to? It had been decades since the boys scrubbed those words off, and yet they had followed him his whole life because of that day. No matter what he did, it wasn't enough to eradicate the memory of that awful priest. The shame that followed.

Already, news of the tiger hunt had reached the tittering tongues of the foreign press. His mentor and benefactor, Hu Jintao, had texted him from China, asking Rajapaksa to save the bones. The skin and whiskers of the tiger could also be used by the Chinese president's aunt in the preparation of traditional Chinese medicine. Rajapaksa ignored the text.

They proceeded straight to the last known place of the tiger: the site of the poor Ondaatje labradoodle's demise. Poor Lucky's fur and bones lay in a stinking pile in Gillian Ondaatje's backyard, flies congregating to feast on its remains. The flies dispersed in dark lines of energy around the hunting party as Rajapaksa poked the remains with a twig. He looked up at poor Gillian, one of his devoted electorate, and mustered up as much steeliness as he could in his too-tight breeches and scarlet coat. "We'll catch the criminal who did this, ma'am," he growled, "Justice will be carried out!"

Gillian nodded and continued weeping into a blue-spotted handkerchief.

The first thing the shikari had them do was to build a traditional trap for the tiger. He found fresh tracks in the nearby forest, although no signs of a kill. This was good news and meant that the tiger would be hungry and ready to kill again. They found a clearing with an area where they could dig a nearby pit. Then they killed a couple of goats and strung them in the branches above the hole. In the hole, they placed a number of sharpened wooden stakes with poison on their tips and then covered the pit with grasses and branches. When the tiger lunged for the bait, it would rip the goats off the branch and then fall into the pit. For good measure, the shikari had men prepare a mixture of mustard oil and latex which was placed around the hole. If the tiger didn't fall in, this mixture would cause him to get leaves and other debris stuck to his paws.

He would then naturally try to pull the sticky debris off using his tongue and teeth, causing the leaves and sticks to get stuck over his eyes. The tiger would go from a terrible beast to a blind duck, panicked and ripe for the shooting. Just to round things off, the shikari had the men build wooden rows of spikes which were attached to the large boles of trees where the tiger had to pass through. Once the tiger was blind, just in case Rajapaksa failed to shoot him, the tiger would be impaled against the side of the trees while trying to run away.

They waited for twelve hours but heard and saw nothing. The goats continued to hang and swing in the hot wind. Flies drew to their sticky blood and the smell was nauseating. Rajapaksa became impatient and charged men to act as beaters. They began burning the surrounding foliage and forest. The shikari assured him that the tiger's tracks they had seen earlier were still fresh and that the great beast was still around. He had a sense for these things. They must wait and be patient.

Rajapaksa chose to ignore him. "Quickly, quickly!" he chided the beaters, "We don't have much time left until the sun sets!"

The men took large bundles of twigs and set them alight, then held them to the foliage and surrounding landscape. In the hot air, the twigs caught fire easily and transmitted their licks of flame to whatever they touched. The fire jumped from tree to tree like a disease. Grass smoked and produced fumes. Heat simmered out of the ground. Flames erupted from the earth. The very fiery cauldron of the earth penetrated through the mantle and set the whole world afire. They could not hear anything for the roars of the flames. The fire was indiscriminate and unappeased, it devoured everything it touched.

Rajapaksa watched with satisfaction as if he were a modern-day Nero, holding a twelve-bore instead of a lyre. If only his brothers could see him! Where were the press and the whinging reporters now?

A few hours later, the fires were still raging. Charred earth and ash filled the horizon. Black clouds of smoke blotted out the sky. The napalmed branches burned to blackened husks and fell in despair and resignation. Animals left the undergrowth in droves. A crocodile came waddling out of a swamp, followed by an axis deer. The screeching of monkeys filled the treetops amongst the cries of mynahs and kingfishers. A cobra slithered out and hissed at Rajapaksa before sliding away. But there was no sign of that great terrorist, the tiger.

Night came and the flames finally began to die down. Alight branches still continued to wither and fall. Rajapaksa and the men had taken care to ensure that the clearing where they had set up the traps would not be touched or encroached upon by the fire. They fought the immediate flames and made for themselves a sort of graveyard of trees with skeletal and charred wood. Denuded of leaves or growth, these charred remains hung tinderous and deathlike around the clearing. They camped there now and could see around them for a couple hundred yards in the twilight. This night, they pulled out the liquor in great quantities. Great jugs of fragrant arrack were passed around and the men drank deeply so that they could ease themselves down onto the smote earth and make of it their smoky beds. And then cautiously, one by one, they fell asleep amongst the singed crackles and the char.

Everyone except Rajapaksa, who remained alert. *No one dares recite Blake this time*, he chuckled to himself. Instead, he commanded a soldier to stay up with him and, to prevent

Rajapaksa from going to sleep, continuously whisper the injunction 'remember the Tamils... remember the Tamils' into his ear like the Persian king Darius was said to have done to rekindle his hatred for the Greeks. Every time Rajapaksa's eyelids began to droop and lower, the soldier, who was somewhat bloated with alcohol and annoyed at not being able to lie down himself, would drunkenly hiss, "remember the Tamils!" Eventually, this soldier and his alcoholic fumes succumbed also and Rajapaksa allowed him to snooze, looking over the rested and content face as it snored between bilious arrack-scented burps. *My electorate,* smiled Rajapaksa fondly to himself, *my people....*

Rajapaksa sensed the tiger before he saw or heard it. The flames had completely died down now and the moonlight fell ghostly and cold through the broken black branches of the night. Silvery light bathed the large beast, three metres long, slinking between the tree trunks and bearing fire and night in its carriage. Sometimes it looked like a being of black fire upon orange fire, at other times orange flames upon black. The black stripes melded with the blackened trunks so that the beast seemed like a floating boulder of darkness and fire. The orange glowed like quartz upon his supple body. His lowered head, hooded eyes, and cautious jaws slightly open, the magnificent body smelled its way towards the goats swinging in the wind.

Making sure that the wind was travelling in the opposite direction, Rajapaksa changed into his breeches and tunic, pulled on the scarlet coat, and swaggered towards his blunderbuss. The pith helmet and the boots came next and clutching the ancient gun, he moved forward on his hands and knees. The elephant was asleep and so were the rest of the men, overfed and drunk. The tiger made his way into the clearing cautiously, and winced when he felt the first spike.

He tested the surface of the trap gently and then seemed to ponder, but then moved forward, picking his way through the centre of the path as gingerly as he could. Rajapaksa marvelled at the might and ability of the tiger to carry such strength yet march so silently.

The tiger waited at the edges of the clearing, sniffing the air, and then circled in a wide radius around the pit. It looked up and then down and gave a soft rumble as if clearing its throat. It circled the edge of the clearing a couple more times. *Could the tiger know what we had prepared?* wondered Rajapaksa.

The tiger looked at the goats swinging in the branches and then scratched the great bole of the tree beneath. There was a great *sccrrrtch* as pieces of bark flew into the air. The tiger sniffed around and found a nearby stump. It crouched upon the stump, peered upwards towards the goats, continually sniffing the air, and then scrunched its nose. Finally, with an almost audible snort of disgust, the tiger turned away from the fly-ridden corpses of the goats, their hides thick with dried blood, and climbed down off the tree trunk. The tiger then began rooting its snout into the stores of food and leftovers from the men's meal. The tiger seemed particularly fond of carrot sambal, licking the plantain leaves clean wherever it could, but it avoided the katta sambal, which was especially hot. Rajapaksa could not believe it! This tiger was a gourmand! He refused the meal of the goats that swung nearby, within easy grasp, but went for the carrot sambal instead. Now that he thought about it, the tiger had eaten only the most delicate and sensitive Tamil and Singhalese children of the villages, the ones who got the highest marks in their classes. This was a very refined tiger indeed!

Clutching his twelve-bore, Rajapaksa sprinted forward to the root of the tree and shook his fist silently at the tiger in fury. He climbed the tree stump which the tiger had vacated, got his bearings, squinted his eye, raised the rifle to his shoulder, remembered to pull instead of squeeze, and then let go a round right into the tiger's haunches.

Next thing he knew, he was flying backwards. He came to, sitting on the ground with what felt like a concussion. Gun smoke hung in the air. The other men woke and slowly realized what was happening. As far as Rajapaksa could tell the tiger was unhurt and still up on its legs, curiously watching the proceedings as the soldiers roused and got themselves dressed. Damned if this blasted bloody tiger was going to make a fool of him and the East India Company! The shikari saw what was going on and tried to stop Rajapaksa but it was too late. Rajapaksa ran up onto the stump, clutching his sprained wrist, and crouched. With some hell-born energy, Rajapaksa leaped like a great lion up into the air and then down onto the back of the tiger. His nails clutched at the tiger's face. His teeth bit into the tiger's neck. His weight crushed the startled beast's back.

The tiger had never been prosecuted in this way before and knew not what to do. It turned its head around and razor-sharp canines stared Rajapaksa in the face. A set of smaller fangs were curled around a hot silent snarl. Eyes that understood death and life and the purest flame of what it was to live, to flicker and die, stared back at him with cruel contempt. A face that could swallow the night hissed hot breath into his nostrils. And then Rajapaksa wet himself. The smell of his urine, as it spread through the fabric of his breeches, making the scarlet of his jacket black, hovered in the cold moonlit air and ran all over the tiger. The smell was an alkali concoction of fear and lime. The tiger sniffed it and, being a clean animal, ran forward. Rajapaksa held on for dear life and wished he could smack the smile off that fearsome beast's face.

But the strain was too much. Already, Rajapaksa with his weight and force had broken the tiger's back, and it crawled forward with much effort and pain. Finally, it gathered all of its strength and momentum and tried to leap. With a weak rustle, the tiger broke free of the ground but soon came down again, falling into the pit. Rajapaksa fell into the pit with it. The branches and grasses gave way and they both fell to the spikes. Luckily for Rajapaksa, the tiger fell first and the poisoned stakes pierced its formidable hide. A soul-piercing cry escaped its jaws and flung itself towards the heavens. Between the tiger and the branches, Rajapaksa was shielded and miraculously incurred only, bruises and scratches which looked a lot worse than they actually were. Grabbing a tree's roots in the earth, he scrambled out of the hole, rabbity, in great panic, and rubbed his hands all over the mustard oil and latex. He then spread it onto his face and cuts. Rajapaksa screamed in agony and tried to pull the leaves and twigs from his eyes. He was blind!

"Get it off me, get it off me!" he cried.

It was the early hours of the dawn by the time they had calmed Rajapaksa down and pulled the latex and leaves from his skin. The soiled coat and breeches were pulled off and thrown away. His cuts were dressed and he remained stripped down to his skivvies and banian. By this time, the tiger had died, the poison taking its course; even in death, the beast looked fearsome and bold. Its legs were splayed in struggle and the terrible eyes were rolled back in agony. They hauled the tiger out and laid the specimen on the ground in front of Rajapaksa. It was measured and weighed. The shikari shook his head. This was not the way things were done. The tiger, despite its fearsome appearance, was old and its muscles were stringy in the daylight. Its flesh hung sallow from its bones. All its fearsome magic seemed to have dissipated with the night.

Rajapaksa and the men worked for hours skinning the beast. They were surprised to see that the stripes extended beyond the fur and were visible in striations upon the skin itself. Rajapaksa hacked off the tail and removed the bones in its tip. He sawed off its feet so that it had no paws and immersed the feet into jars containing a palm oil solution. He cut its whiskers and scattered them on the ground.

Slowly, using a large carving knife, Rajapaksa disemboweled the tiger, removing first its kidneys, spleen, and liver which he placed in the grass beside the dead body to drain, their fluids soaking out while their membranes became bloated and thin. He then sawed away at those mighty ribs, breaking the sternum and crushing the rib cage so that they matched the spinal cord which had been shattered earlier. The mighty heart, the engine of the terrible beast, lay in his hands, a deflated pump, having pushed its last tide of blood hours ago, now a sac without life. He bit into the raw heart and chewed its flesh thoughtfully. It retained the toughness of old beef and its taste was bitter, although not unpleasant. This was a moment he had waited for a long time and the soldiers, still somewhat hungover and fried from the adrenalin, looked aside with disgust. The lungs were cut out and flung back into the clearing. They landed near the elephant and it retreated as if the alveoli still exhaled oxygen. Rajapaksa reached up and under the crushed rib cage. He squeezed the tiger's trachea and crushed its voice box, ensuring it could not speak after death and come back to haunt him.

The other men had staked the eviscerated skin to the ground. It looked as if its life had spread out into a puddle, and was slowly beginning to ooze into the ground, leaving nothing but a dry husk. They began filing away at the tiger's teeth. These would be war trophies and the largest fangs would go to Rajapaksa and his clan. Rajapaksa patted the tiger now lovingly on its stripped cheek. Without his whiskers, the tiger was almost a large pussycat, fit only for slinking around the house. Rajapaksa then thrust his forefingers into the cat's eyeballs and pulled the dead glassy orbs out of their sockets. The eyes were hard and resistant and he had to use a short knife to sever the optic nerve from the skull. He squished the vile jelly in his palms and licked the bloody juices which ran down the sides of his hands. His sprained wrist still hurt but that only made the act more precious. What sweetness in victory! What sweetness in life! He bent down and cut off the tiger's limp penis with a final flourish of the knife and then flung this so far into the forest that all the animals would inevitably see what a weak and pathetic and shrivelled thing it was to be a tiger.

The men joined in on the fun. They shattered the tiger's jaw with the butt of Rajapaksa's gun and smashed its nose for good measure. The ancient W & J Kavanagh firearm bashed in the remains of the tiger's skull until it was broken and bloody. The brains, wet grey and pink drizzle, oozed out through the leaky cranium, its crushed ears, and open mouth. With its toothless gums and hollow smile, the tiger still mocked them slightly. It maintained a battered sneer, even beyond death. Thinking of the leonine priest from Sigiriya rock all those years ago, Rajapaksa took the stock of his gun back from the soldiers and brought it down upon the tiger's shattered skull again and again and again.

Then, when the tiger was destroyed, its parts broken and its maw mangled, Rajapaksa finally relaxed and let go his weapons. A strange calm descended over him, his mind became purified. He crouched down and removing the stakes, wrapped himself in the skinned tiger pelt that lay bloody and raw on the grass. He pulled it tightly over his body as if it were a royal bed sheet. The blood and the smell did not bother him. The guts and the matted hair did not seem to take away the pleasure. In fact, they only added to it. He smeared the blood all over his face.

Rajapaksa went to sleep right there, like a baby, and slept the best sleep he had slept in many days.

Katta Sambal

Look at Mahinda sleeping! Isn't he a darling? I've been told that his face is one that only a mother could love. Even smeared with blood, it fills me with love. Look at the way his moustache rises and falls!

I'm sorry; I was taken away there for a while. Now, you're probably wondering what exactly is this katta sambal that the tiger avoided? And what kind of self-respecting tiger would avoid a dish because it's too hot? The tiger should be ashamed to consider himself Tamil! Someone should rub his tummy and ask him if he has an upset stomach!

Ingredients:
5 dried chilies
1 tablespoon Maldive fish
1 teaspoon salt
½ a lime

Take the chilies, salt, and the Maldive fish and grind them in a mortar and pestle. The Maldive fish is a cured tuna from the Maldives but if you're having a hard time finding it, you can substitute prawns or shrimp instead. Squeeze in the lime juice and gently mix it all together. Squint your eyes, slather your tongue with lots of saliva, and keep a big cool glass of water handy – enjoy!

Dream of Mahinda

Mahinda Rajapaksa took tea with his newly appointed Secretary of Mass Media, Charitha Herath. Herath had not touched his tea yet and fiddled with a stack of dossiers, clipped articles, and e-mail printouts. Two sugar cubes still sat on his saucer, unstirred, and the man's sleepy eyes belied a nervous cough. Rajapaksa had always been suspicious of men whose complexions were too light; he looked at the Minister's large ears and acorn-shaped head, waved him to go on.

"What other news?" he asked the secretary as he stirred his own tea with a stick of cinnamon, which was taking an impossibly long time to soften. He liked the cinnamon because it was so hard and tart.

"Some offers from India," replied Herath, coughing into his right fist and riffling through the printed e-mails.

"No need to show me. Just tell me about it."

"Well, I informed them you probably weren't interested, but one of the larger networks proposed doing a big big reality TV show with Gota, your brother."

"Oh yes?" *Why not me?* thought Rajapaksa.

"It's not something you'd want to do," stated Herath boldly. He had read Rajapaksa's mind and realizing he had been too forward, dialled backwards on himself and simpered appeasingly: "They want to make it like *The Apprentice* in America with Donald Trump. They would call it *The Fourth Estate* and journalists would compete to write a story on current events. They would compete each week, overseen by Gota, and if he didn't like what they wrote, he'd fire them. One by one, they're all fired and the lone winner, with Ministry approval, gets to publish his article. It's nonsense. The catchphrase they want to use is 'You're censored!' Mark my words. Nothing will come of it."

Rajapaksa enjoyed being courted by foreign interests. Countries such as India, Russia, and China were forever flirting and currying favour. It made him feel virginal, like a girl in one of those American high school movies, vied over by many boys for the high school prom. *As if he had not had his cherry popped yet!*

"Okay. What else?" he asked.

"There's a network that wants to do another type of reality show. They want to call it *Tamil Activist Babes* and it's a cross between *Real Housewives* and *Idol*. Big big ratings. They'll interview Tamil activists that live abroad like M.I.A., Meena Kandasamy, Niromi De Soyza, people like that, and they'll compete against each other weekly in terms of things like: level of activism, most diverse entourage, best singing voice, and, last but not least, prettiest sari."

"What do they want to do with us?" asked Rakapaksa irritably.

"They want rights to broadcast in Sri Lanka."

"Definitely not!" stammered Rajapaksa, grinding his cinnamon stick into the bottom of his teacup and splashing the tea everywhere. The liquid flew up and sprayed across Herath's face and shirt, got lost in the jungle of his hair. Herath excused himself and wiped his face with a satin handkerchief. "You've got some on your earth-coloured shawl, sir," he observed, offering Rajapaksa the handkerchief.

Rajapaksa took the piece of cloth and dabbed at his shawl. "It's not earth, it's kurakkan. Earth is black or brown. It's not really red, is it?"

"It is in the North and the East," grinned Herath with a glint in his eye, referring to all the bloodshed that had happened there.

The two broke out in laughter and Rajapaksa had to touch his eyes with the shawl. Perhaps Herath wasn't so bad after all....

The shawl reminded him of his uncle D. M., the Lion of Ruhuna, who had worn a similar political stole. The years before his father died, Rajapaksa had been working in a library, finishing his studies, and entertained fantasies of becoming a matinee idol. He had not really considered politics seriously then – it seemed like many lifetimes ago – even though his father had suffered greatly after defeat in '65 and had to sell the car and lease the family lands. In the mid-sixties, Rajapaksa believed in the power of cinema to cure all woes; it lifted the hearts of rich and poor alike, and he would never have thought that one person should pick and choose to decide what the people see. If he had been asked then, he would have thought that all censorship should be prohibited forever. It was a free and innocent time. He was lucky now to have Gota take care of that dirty business for him; Gota always took the brunt of the blame and it was getting to him, Rajapaksa could tell, but better that than ruffle his own soft-spoken image. If the public knew what Gota had been like as a teenager with the mice! They had been young once... the feelings were coming back to him now... he wanted to be this nation's darling, the Singhalese Sean Connery rivalling the superstardom of Dev Anand and Raj Kapoor.

There was a time when he had the chance. He was contracted, mostly through his father's connections, to play a monk in a film called *Dream of Dharmapala* starring Gamini Fonseka and directed by L. J. Peries. The film had been doomed from the start. To save money, the film was to be shot using a small village near the Vanni. The heat was unbearable and the local Tamils came to gawk and snicker. What constituted the film's tale, which had already brought great local opprobrium and controversy, was a reworking of the story of Dharmapala. Rajapaksa was to play a young would-be monk torn between following Dharmapala and falling in love and marrying a local girl. The local girl was played by Maggie Fernando, a young actress who had never been in anything else. She was from the capital and like Rajapaksa, had gotten the role through connections. Maggie was often demanding and belligerent on set. Whatever she came from, she already thought herself a star. Though Rajapaksa normally did not like women like that, he found her curiously alluring. Most women he met through school or at the occasional party laughed at him: he was a little portly and wore his moustaches awkwardly. He knew that was why he had been given the minor supporting comedic role. His film dialogue with Maggie during takes would run like this:

Rajapaksa: But I am torn, don't you see?

Maggie: Are you a piece of paper to be torn so easily? I don't want to be seen talking to a coward.

Rajapaksa: But I love you, and you're never home when I call on the telephone.

Maggie: What am I? A telephone operator to sit by the phone all day?

Rajapaksa: I would die without you!

Maggie: Then you must be a ghost to be standing here: a hungry ghost come back from the dead. Looking at your gut, I would say a *very* very hungry ghost!

(And so on it went.)

Though she was difficult, Maggie had great flashing eyes, gales of emotion pouring from her face. Her legs were short and sturdy and her breasts strained against the blouse of her sari. When they were dancing together during the musical numbers, he found it impossible not to hold her tightly, pressing his fingers against her round hips, feeling the thrust of her pelvis under the sheer fabric, knowing that the dip of her navel was only inches away.

He could remember the afternoon of his last day on the film, the jungle heat blasting like a furnace, when Maggie screamed that he was grabbing her too much and stopped the take.

"You're supposed to indicate your love," said Peries, gently, "not consummate it. Leave something to the audience's imagination, dear boy."

"And he should tighten his monk's robe," shrieked Maggie, "his robe is also leaving too little to the imagination!"

Everyone was used to Maggie's tirades and humoured her. Rajapaksa had not had much experience with headstrong women and he felt awkward around them. On the first day of shooting their scenes together, Maggie had said aloud that if Rajapaksa were a monk, he should not keep his moustache. She said that his moustache looked like two large hairy caterpillars that had climbed up his face and met in the middle and were now in each other's way, yet neither one wanted to do the gracious thing and retreat. Another time, she had said that a monkey, grabbing onto his moustache like a handlebar and sitting on his head, could act his part for him and do a better job. She told him that he should stick to crossing parliamentary floors because that's all his family was good for.

"He's a pervert," she screamed now, "not even the Buddha would have compassion for him!"

Peries' assistant called a break while somebody went over and placated Maggie. Rajapaksa retired to a corner, where they kept a cot for him, to give her some space.

He lay down, trying not to wrinkle the folds of his robe. The heat was a furnace's flames blowing over him. Instead of a sea breeze, it was as if the island were surrounded by a sea of fire that blew gusts of heat over the land. Tired, exhausted, he dropped off to sleep and imagined himself on a cool night in a clearing in the forest. He was in his orange robe but no one else from the film crew was there. Overhead, the stars twinkled beautifully in a sky as dark and starkly negative as unexposed film. He felt the ground shake and quiver. The grasses around his bare feet and legs rustled. A breeze blew over him, ruffling the folds of his robe.

Something sat up from the ground, eased itself languorously, propped itself on a lazy elbow. It was hard to see in the dark but now the thing got up and shimmered and danced and rocked its hips, walked towards him and around him. It was a woman and she walked with the drowsy air of someone he had made love to. She was uncurling for the second round. But this was like no woman he had ever seen before. Her face was smooth and powdery as sand; the mouth and the lips formed of seashells. Her strong sturdy limbs were made of coconut wood and when she spoke, he felt drunk, as if from arrack. Her joints and sinews were rubbery and fertile, her breasts a loamy mass of tea leaves and earth. Rubies glinted in her eyes. She was covered with moss and vegetation and possessed grass instead of hair.

"Who are you?" he asked, wonderstruck.

"Why, I'm your lover," she replied with intoxicating sighs. "Don't you recognize me?"

He knew what she was then and came to her, grabbing the Adam's Peak of her breasts, snuffling the cool leaves of her Hill Country, grinding his loins into the steamy humid Vanni between her thighs. He knew who she was and she would be all the lover he needed. He would grind himself into her day and night; again and again and again. He would plunder her, leave her spent and dried.

Somewhere below them, the surf pounded beyond the forest. He could hear the spray relentlessly hitting the rock, again and again in his ears. Maggie Fernando was down there and he could just barely hear her voice whispering in the wind: *not even the Buddha would forgive what you do!*

Rajapaksa was woken that day from his dream by Peries' assistant who said, "We're filming again in ten minutes."

As Rajapaksa sat up, they both glanced down at the folds of his robe below his belly and saw a series of stains that covered his legs. The stains were dark against the orange robe and formed an archipelago down his left thigh, the topmost blob looking like an upside-down Ceylon. For a moment, Rajapaksa and the assistant were puzzled; then the distinctive, sweet, queasy smell left no doubt. "Hold on," cried the assistant back to the film crew, "Rajapaksa's had nocturnal emissions again. We'll have to wait until they wash the robe!"

Everyone groaned and fanned themselves, went to fetch some soft drinks. He could just imagine what Maggie would say about all this.

They fired him the next day and he had to phone back home to Hambantota to tell the family. His brother Gota, in his late teens, answered the phone. Rajapaksa asked his brother how things had been going lately. It had been a particularly bad year since their father had lost the election and the inability to make ends meet showed up in the most curious of ways. Gota told him that mice had gotten into the house. Some people they had leased their land to had been conducting heavy digging and the mice had scurried out of the field and into the house.

"What are you going to do?" asked Rajapaksa.

"I'm going to smoke the bloody buggers out," replied his brother with a maniacal smile he could see clearly as if he stood in front of him.

"You're going to smoke out the mice with fire?" asked Rajapaksa, forgetting his own troubles. "Don't you think that's too drastic?"

"Listen – the mice are chewing through the cables; some especially rebellious ones are sabotaging the lights. I can't listen to the radio."

"What if you burn down the house?"

"I'll use dynamite if I have to! Don't you know me?"

"Dynamite?!" exclaimed Rajapaksa in alarm, "What will the neighbours say?"

"We'll just tell them they're mistaken, they didn't hear anything, false rumours spread by people who are sympathetic to mice, I'll think of something...."

Rajapaksa hung up the phone in disbelief, forgetting to convey the news about his return home. It was just as well. The production near the Vanni was abandoned when some Tamils (they never found out who) sabotaged the equipment by pouring sand into the cameras. His father died the following year and Rajapaksa replaced him as SLFP candidate. His interest in films waned and he was gripped by a newfound thirst for politics that he couldn't quite explain.

Rajapaksa leaned back now and stirred the fresh cup of tea that Herath had provided. "What are you waiting for?" he asked.

"For my handkerchief, sir, are you finished with it?"

Rajapaksa realized he was still holding the piece of cloth and gave it back. He wondered where Maggie Fernando was now. He amused himself with the thought of having Gota find her and abduct her before torturing and scaring her a little bit. But then they would let her go; it would only be in good fun. *No, no, let it go*, he thought to himself. *Let the mice run and have their little scraps.*

He fancied that he could hear a scratching beneath the baseboards now, a low *whirr-whirr*. Did Herath also hear the noise? He didn't want to be suspected of hearing things and so could not ask. Herath would not say anything, would only look back at him with a cocked sleepy eyebrow, a nervous cough, waiting to tell all the others about it. *Mahinda's going the way of his brother! Can you believe it?* Little mice nibbling at each other. Let them have their scraps. *Whirr-whirr.* There was the noise again – surely Herath heard it now? Yet he could not say anything, waited for Herath to break the silence, imagined their rodent incisors gnawing through the wood and cables. How funny it was where the mice could get to!

Coconut Lentil Curry

In the following story, there is a mention of crab curry – a Sri Lankan favourite. If for some reason you're vegetarian (perhaps the Buddhist masters are looking over your shoulder while you eat), or you're worried about mercury poisoning, try substituting a coconut lentil curry instead.

Ingredients:
½ cup of orange lentils
½ an onion, sliced
5 cloves of garlic, halved
½ teaspoon of turmeric
½ teaspoon Sri Lankan raw curry powder
2 green chilies, split down the middle
2 stalks of curry leaves
2 cinnamon sticks
1 cup of coconut milk
½ cup of water
¼ teaspoon of salt
pepper (to taste)

My goodness, what a lot of ingredients! Now I remember why people prefer to do the crab curry! Okay, we'd better begin as soon as we can. Wash the lentils thoroughly with water. Throw the washed lentils into a pot and then add the onions, garlic, turmeric, curry powder, coconut milk, water, salt, and pepper. Cook this over low heat for about 15 mins., until the lentils become yellow. Then add the chilies, curry leaves, and cinnamon sticks. Stir everything around once. Close the pot and allow it to simmer for 5 mins.

Celluloid Visions

Rajapaksa was mad and he wasn't going to take it any more. He was sick of all the people, his people, who questioned his government's decisions. He was sick of the journalists who wagged their censorious fingers. He was sick of his own family who embarrassed him. Didn't they know what he was trying to do out here? You try to do something great and nobody appreciates it. Rajapaksa was staying near the port in Hambantota for the weekend. The traffic in the port functioned beautifully and on a clear day, you could almost see straight to Madagascar.

He sat up in bed now, late at night, with the brand new 10G laptop and mobile internet stick, a small gift from the powers that be in China. He *was* looking for YouTube clips of the Sri Lankan team at the London Olympics. What he found was footage of British Tamils protesting, waving their cursed red flag with the stupid face of their tiger on it. *What, are the doughnut shops closed? Don't you have anywhere to go?* Rajapaksa thought irritably to himself. "What do we want? Justice! What do we want? Justice!" chanted the Tamils again and again, reminding Rajapaksa of his futile time at the hotel in London. "This isn't a Sai Baba bajan, you fools!" he muttered aloud, "think of something original to say!"

The large frame of his wife turned slowly and spoke with a croaking voice, "Go to sleep, Mahinda, it's late... put that thing away."

"Don't tell me what to do, Miss Lanka '73," muttered Rajapaksa and shook off her cloying arm.

It was true. Since the Chinese had given him this laptop with the extremely fast Intel Core processor, 10G memory, and dozens of applications unavailable in Sri Lanka, he and the laptop had been inseparable. It was amazing what the Chinese could do. He only wished that they had listened and given him one in kurakkan, the same colour as his shawl (he believed in matching accessories). Instead, they had given him one with a red skin, the stars of the Chinese flag flying in the corner; even the internet stick was red. It bothered him that a few years after defeating the threat of one red flag, another should attach itself to him so easily. Ruhunu Magampura International Port, paid for by the Chinese, would be the most beautiful port in the world. There was even a separate dock for secret arms shipments. But what did the future hold? He imagined every building flying a red flag and a harbour full of Chinese junks. The Orientals with their dragon festivals and ping-pong champions and opium dens would be running the place. He saw the population of Sri Lanka slaving in sweatshops for pennies, fabricating cheap cellphones and dollar store items. And exactly *how* did he feel about Chinese food — wasn't that the real question?

He had to master his use of laptop time. Technology had pitfalls too; at various times, he had become addicted to internet gambling, eBay India, illegal downloading, and World of Warcraft. Sometimes, he would log on to Match.com, posing as a Tamil woman, and then flirt with Tamil men so that he could then break their hearts. On other nights, when he couldn't sleep, he needed to watch a little porn before he could doze off. Once, he had started out looking for the fabled Aishwarya Rai sex tape but ended up with all kinds of articles and outrage at his brother Gotabaya's comments regarding the woman in the Channel 4 documentary. He and Shiranthi tried to deal with his brother's indiscretions by talking to him the next day but he should have known better. They had Gota over to lunch and Gota could barely restrain himself.

"What? Whenever I see a pretty girl, I wonder whether she's been raped or not. Isn't that normal?" asked Gota, as if innocent.

"Idiot!" hissed Rajapaksa, and smacked his brother against the ear. Probably, if left to his own devices, Gota would be like some brown Benny Hill, chasing SriLankan Airlines stewardesses up and down the country. "Women are there to be married, not to be raped," added Rajapaksa.

His wife had gotten up in disgust, snorting as she fussed around in the background.

"What's *your* problem?" he had asked her later.

"Sometimes I don't know why I married into this family. I'd gather the boys and leave if I didn't know that you'd have me killed."

"You have a firm grasp on our relationship," he chuckled dryly.

Now, before going to sleep, he checked in with the LTTE rehabilitation camp through Skype. Being able to video conference for free meant that they could save on the telecommunication bills. After being tortured for information, the captured Tiger cadres were subjected to a technique of aversion therapy. The boys were strapped into a chair with their eyelids pried open (the idea had come from a Kubrick film of the seventies) and forced to watch Tamil movies. Thus, their association with anything remotely Tamil was broken down and came to provoke disgust and nausea if they encountered any reminders.

The sleepy-eyed lieutenant on the other end of the video conference saluted him and told him that everything proceeded smoothly. Always, in Sri Lanka, everything was proceeding smoothly. Rajapaksa could hear the jangle of a Tamil movie's musical number in the background and the throaty, strident, complicated vowels always made his eardrums grind. He closed down the video chat as soon as possible. Was this the best way to proceed? Could they effect the same changes without using Tamil movies? Psychological studies showed that positive reinforcement was always stronger than negative reinforcement techniques. Could there be another way? He finally turned off the laptop and went to sleep, ruminating.

*

Rajapaksa came up with a brilliant solution once he was back in the capital. In the eighties, the Turkish film industry had produced a number of rip-offs of American films. Big in Turkey at the time, they appropriated the larger-than-life stories of films like *E.T.* and *Star Wars*, and India had followed suit with re-workings of blockbusters as diverse as *Mrs. Doubtfire* and *Terminator*. Why not do that in Sri Lanka? The American Empire, during its height, had been propelled by the jingoism and boosterism of its film industry. He would take its mightiest classics and make Singhalese adaptations using unprecedented production levels. They would be tested on the deprogrammed Tamils first and then released to wider audiences later.

So he started a film club. He forced Herath and other ministers to sit with him and they watched great American films presented to them by a lecturer from the University of Peradeniya Film Society. Regardless of the movies they watched, the classic films would begin to jog Rajapaksa's feelings and desires of wanting to be a major film star. His long-abandoned dreams brought a fresh poignant sting to the viewings that he had not anticipated. He couldn't help but imagine himself in the lead roles.

They began with the early talkies. The first film was *The Wizard of Oz*. Rajapaksa imagined himself as Dorothy in a gingham dress and cute pigtails. Toto, trustingly and lovingly held in his arms, was the Sri Lankan electorate and they were trying to get back home, to a country before the shrill troublemakers and dissidents had pulled it apart. They followed the yellow brick road, which he surmised would represent Chinese and Oriental influences, to the Emerald City, a time of prosperity and wealth which made Sri Lanka the jewel of the Indian Ocean. By that analogy, the Wicked Witch of the North and East was Prabhakaran. The Good Witches were probably Iran and Libya. The ministers listened patiently to his analogies. The Lion represented the Singhalese, of course, the Scarecrow represented the Muslims because they were always running scared, and the Tin Man was the Christians because they had no heart. Who were the Tamils? Why, they could be the Flying Monkeys, ruled over by the Wicked Witch. At this point, his metaphors became mixed. What were the sparkly red shoes? They were a pair of glittering long-range neutron bombs from China that could be deployed on the North and the East.

"But the lion is cowardly," objected one of the ministers.

"The truth is that the Singhalese *are* a little cowardly," rebuffed Rajapaksa with an offhand air. That quickly shut them up.

He stroked an imaginary Cairn Terrier while he remembered the Central Bank bombing in Colombo of '96. Few people knew this but Rajapaksa had been there at a catered lunch on the premises. There had been a second suicide bomber besides the initial one who had driven the lorry through the main gate. This second bomber wore a plastics explosive belt and burst into the central manager's office where Rajapaksa and others had been enjoying a three course meal of confit ocean trout and crab curry with vegetables and dessert. When the suicide bomber burst in, disguised as an SLA regular, Rajapaksa had immediately known what the intruder was. The lean and bony frame, the emaciated face, told him everything. For a moment, the bomber dawdled, staring at the heaps of food in front of him. Rajapaksa saw the hungry look in his eyes, could see the bomber pause to reflect, thinking that having lived on a spoonful of rice a day, Rajapaksa's plate alone could feed an entire platoon.

Rajapaksa had sprung into action then. "Don't worry, leave it to me, sir!" he cried and while the bomber still stood there, shocked, Rajapaksa grabbed as much food onto his plate as he could and ran out. He had been courageous and done the right thing. He had not let the terrorists take away his food. Seconds later, a lorry and three-wheeler had crashed through the gate and the bomber ignited his load in the manager's office. Rajapaksa had heroically escaped with second-degree burns and most of the food.

"Well, food for thought," mused Rajapaksa hungrily, "what else do we have?"

They watched that great milestone of the seventies, *The Godfather*. Once again, Rajapaksa could not but help think of himself as Michael, Al Pacino with his nasal voice and intent gaze. He thought of his father, D. A., as the elder godfather, holding the dynasty together with force of character and aplomb, dying of ill health, fatigue, and sadness. Gota was like Sonny, then, with his wild temper and manic outbursts. By that reckoning, Basil was Fredo with his round face and lecherous eyes. Rajapaksa was Michael through and through, not wanting to get into the family business and then forced by circumstances to intervene; only he had the will and mental acuity to rescue their faltering hopes and save the family honour.

Rajapaksa re-imagined the scene at the restaurant which would play out like one of the many failed peace talks between the Sri Lankan government and the LTTE. The oblivious cop bodyguard, ostensibly there for protection and moderation, was the Norwegian government. If Rajapaksa had been there, he would have asked to go to the bathroom immediately, having endured Prabhakaran frisking his crotch, and then retrieved the pistol and blown the heads off the LTTE and foreign interference. *Absolutely correct.* He was going to make the Tamils an offer they couldn't refuse. Tonight, the Rajapaksa family would settle all its accounts. Only, he would have packed up the leftovers on the table before leaving. He didn't believe in wasting food.

He wondered if he could hire Al Pacino to fly over and teach Rajapaksa to act like him. It was a masterful performance. Some of Michael's wisdom might even have rubbed off permanently onto Pacino and he could ask the great actor what he should do in the current situation with Gota. It wasn't Gota's fault, really. Rajapaksa knew that some of the blame for the way Gota was rested on him and the other brothers. When they were children, Rajapaksa had always sought to embarrass and quash Gota's enthusiasm by humiliating him. The other brothers rallied around and took no end to teasing and mocking their short brother. Flighty and excitable, Gota was always the last to be selected for soccer tournaments. A brother might shake a soft drink vigorously and then offer it to the unsuspecting Gota, and then laugh when the drink exploded all over his face and shirt. Then their father would beat Gota. Once, Basil and the others held Gota down in the dust whilst Rajapaksa squatted over Gota and farted onto his face. Wave after wave of Rajapaksa flatus assailed the unfortunate Gota's nostrils but Gota could not turn away. His head had been held in place like the deprogrammed LTTE cadres. It had made his younger brother sullen, despondent, and enraged. Rajapaksa had offered him the Secretary of Defense position years later partly out of guilt.

The third film they watched that day was considered to be the greatest American film of the eighties and it disturbed Rajapaksa greatly. *Raging Bull* was not like the others. With its unabashed swearing forming a gritty taste and texture throughout the script, the black-and-white film presented its characters in unglamourous terms. Robert De Niro played real life boxer Jake LaMotta and Joe Pesci his brother, Joey. Jake was a ferocious, uncouth animal and the film was set both inside and outside the ring. With his strange tics and rugged face, De Niro brooded an intensity like no other actor; he was unattractive but mesmerizing. Joe Pesci was like Gota, short and stubby and excitable, but was Rajapaksa like De Niro? Did he want to be? Prabhakaran was like Sugar Ray Robinson in the film, dark and inhuman and demonized in the key sequences that framed their matches.

That image of De Niro at the end... having pushed away his family and friends, squandered his fortune... De Niro had actually put on a mass of weight for those scenes; it was not a fat suit. He sat there, bloated, wasted, and aged, smoking a cigar while reciting bad lines for a nightclub set, ruminating on all the mistakes he had made. The sad old LaMotta stared at himself in the mirror and pummelled the air, repeating the mantra "I'm the boss... I'm the boss."

It was not a role that Rajapaksa wanted but it haunted him, the performances and the melancholy unrelenting film. The next day, Rajapaksa had Gota come into his office and he presented his younger brother with a copy of the script.

Without much in the way of preparation, Rajapaksa had Gota read a scene from the script with himself reading De Niro's lines while Gota read Pesci's. They turned to page 138 at random.

Rajapaksa: Did you fuck my wife?

Gota: What?

Rajapaksa: (*quietly*) Did you fuck my wife?

Gota: How could you ask me a question like that? How could you ask me? I'm your brother. You ask me that? Where do you get your balls big enough to ask me that?

Rajapaksa: Just tell me.

Gota: I'm not answering. I'm not gonna answer that. It's stupid.

Rajapaksa: You're very smart, Gota (*he improvised that part*). You're givin' me all these answers but you ain't givin' me the right answer. I'm gonna ask you again. Did you or did you not?

Gota: I'm not gonna answer. It's a sick question. You're a sick fuck, and I'm not that sick that I'm gonna answer it. I'm not telling ya anything. I'm gonna leave so if Lenore calls, tell her I went home. I'm not staying in this nuthouse 'cause you're a sick bastard. I feel sorry for you, I really do. You know what you should do? Try a little more fucking and a little less eating. You won't have troubles upstairs in your bedroom and you won't take it out on me and everybody else... you understand, you fucking wacko? You're cracking up!

At this point, Gota broke character and said, "What's the meaning of this filth? What is this?"

Rajapaksa then, without planning to, slapped his brother. His brother looked back at him, stunned.

"Why did you do that?" Gota raised a hand to his cheek and broke into tears, sobbing. He threw the script onto the desk and ran out of Rajapaksa's office. Whoever was due to meet with his brother for the rest of the day would probably be subject to the extent of Gota's rancour and wrath. It couldn't be helped. The script, the film, had done something to Rajapaksa. It seized him. *He was alive!* He felt more powerful, more sensitive, more vulnerable than ever before. It was as if each pore was bursting with emotion, as if pain and intensity were oozing out of his skin.

That night, while his wife slept, Rajapaksa stayed up with the red laptop. He read all the articles and the rants and the objections and the complaints against him from places as far-flung as the UK, Canada, Australia, and the States. They were relentless and unflinching and Rajapaksa felt as if he were being pummelled by a thousand boxers, simultaneously, in the ring. Unforgivingly, they dished it out and he took it to prove that he could. He even welcomed it.

Towards the end of his reading, at the point of despair when he felt he might crack and not be able to take it anymore, he saw a Google ad in the corner for something called The Kids Helpline. The helpline promised twenty-four hour online counselling to poor victims who had been bullied through a variety of means, including something called online bullying where a bunch of anonymous perpetrators picked on and harassed a single victim. This was the first time Rajapaksa had heard the term. An operator was standing by to IM with him in real time.

Rajapaksa logged on with a fake name just to be safe and talked to the operator:

Operator: Hello?

Singha956: Hi.

Operator: Hello, thank you for being brave enough to reach out and talk to someone. Now, the first thing I have to ask you is: have you been inappropriately touched by someone?

Singha956: No... I don't think so.

Operator: What's happened then? Tell me about it.

Singha956: There are all these people on the internet making fun of me and calling me names.

Operator: You mean on Facebook and Tumblr and things like that? What are they saying?

Singha956: They're saying that I'm guilty of genocide and war crimes, that I curtail media freedom, and that I oversee a corrupt regime that controls over 70% of the country's finances.

Operator: Wait... what? How old are you?

At this point, Rajapaksa slammed the laptop shut. Beads of perspiration rained down his face and he wondered for a moment whether they could trace the IM conversation. Another scandal was all he really needed right now. Wouldn't it be better to just hack into all the sites that printed declamatory articles and erase them? How long would it take? Did they even have anybody who was smart enough to do that? The internet stick, stuck in the side of the laptop, continued to glow. A red light flashed, sending out a wireless signal to Beijing. Could it be, could it be they were aware of everything he was doing, everything he was thinking? Or was that too paranoid?

He sat up, unable to get to sleep, and whispered to himself softly, "I'm the boss... I'm the boss."

Hoppers

Yes, Mahinda, you're the boss, forever and always. My Mahinda was always more fond of movies than books. He was what you could call a 'movie man.' Someone should make a movie of his life.

In fact, through working at a library, he came to hate books and what they stood for. When the Sri Lankan army burned down the Jaffna library, Mahinda said, "Those Tamils should stop crying and look on the bright side. Now, at least, they won't have to pay their overdue fines!"

Let's make some hoppers and distract ourselves from such depressing matters! Hoppers are a classic staple of Sri Lankan breakfast and I challenge anyone who tries this sweet toasted milky treat to not fall in love with it instantly! Forget that Roman rubbish they're all eating in the next story – if they had hoppers in Rome, perhaps their empire *would* have lasted forever.

Ingredients:
2 cups of rice flour
2 cans of coconut milk
¼ teaspoon of instant yeast
2 teaspoons of sugar
¼ teaspoon of salt

Take all of the ingredients, except the salt and coconut milk, and mix them together. Leave the mixture to settle overnight. The next day, add the coconut milk and salt into the pot and mix everything together into a thick batter. Pour a batch of the final butter into a hot hopper pan and cover it with a lid. When the hopper is brown and crispy, about 5 mins. later, it is ready to be removed and eaten.

Oh, it looks like Don Alvin makes an appearance in this next story. Remember: don't tell him that you saw me...

The New Rome

Rajapaksa and his brothers (Gota, Basil, and Chamal) walked up the magnificent steps of the Old Parliament Building. With its ionic columns and classical pediment, it reminded Rajapaksa of some ancient Roman temple. The ceremonial guards and security saluted Rajapaksa and his brothers, then quickly ran away. It was May and time for another bacchanalian feast. Another Victory Day parade had gone splendidly and now it was time for the Rajapaksas to celebrate in private, where they could role play and drop their studied and solemn facades. The three lesser Rajapaksa brethren trooped up the steps with a jaunty gait, wearing the rich wool togas of Roman senators. Stripes on their hems symbolized status. Rajapaksa was being carried and wore the laurels of an emperor. Tamil servants, made up to look like Ethiopian slaves – or 'darkies' as the jovial brothers fondly referred to them – heaved Rajapaksa on a bamboo litter draped with a lion's skin. Women with fitted gold bangles around their necks fanned him as the procession of brothers, their retinue of slaves, and a reluctant soothsayer made their way up the steps.

Rajapaksa only wished that his dearest brother, little Dudley, could be there. Dudley had been the favourite of their father's when the old man had been alive and because of that, there seemed to be a halo around his younger brother that the other Rajapaksas could not penetrate. An innocence and love surrounded Dudley, an aloof purity that superseded even the little girls in the family. The other brothers, Gotabaya and Basil, had returned eagerly from the States to take up their positions of power in Rajapaksa's government but their predictability and eagerness only made the president disdain his brothers even more, despite their supposed loyalty. Only Dudley had remained untouched and pure. This purity, made sharper through years of denial of that particular event at Sigiriya rock, had now been shattered.

It was true that since he had been given a powerful laptop by the Chinese, Rajapaksa sometimes went on to Match.com, posing as a Tamil woman so that he could flirt with Tamil men and break their hearts. He had a playful, tricksterish side. Heavy was the burden of Sri Lanka's crown and the role play gave him release. He had taken great care with his profile and even scoured the internet for photos of an anonymous dark Tamil beauty, a sari model, that he could use for his own profile. He liked the tease of messaging back and forth, the slow burn of IM chat windows in which more was implied than said. He honed his skills at charming the eager hordes of Tamils out there, still alive in the world. It wasn't technically what you would call 'cheating', even though his wife Shiranthi knew nothing about it. Shiranthi and other women had been especially difficult to him as a younger man and so this was his revenge, his way to turn the tables and reverse the roles. Could anyone blame him for having a little fun?

The problem was that, unbeknownst to Rajapaksa, Dudley also went on to Match.com without his family or anyone else knowing. Dudley, pure and noble Dudley, posed as a Tamil man, not because he wanted to beguile or charm but because he had a genuine desire to see how the other half lived: he wanted to know what it was to be a Tamil man. He felt slightly guilty for having been born Singhalese and a Rajapaksa. While the other brothers had their mayhem and fun, looting and killing the country, Dudley felt compassion, suffered with the victims as the Buddha has taught us to do. What the Buddha has not taught us, however, is to log on to Match.com under an assumed identity. This was purely Dudley's idea.

The two brothers, Mahinda and Dudley, innocent of the true perils and dark fate that awaited them, met anonymously in cyberspace. They flirted as Tamil man and woman, assuming a mantle of love which goes back to the Dravidian beginnings of time. Rajapaksa usually prided himself on taking his victims to the point of no return, a vapid horizon where his victims were ready to propose to him... and then came the torturous break – he broke their dreams with a delectably swift and callous rejection. He remained positively cruel. Rajapaksa had become a breakup artist who subtly intoxicated his victims like a venomous spider, dissolving their wills into his web, enticing them with a mixture of coquettishness and flattery and then injecting the poison of denial. The further he could carry the seduction, the greater the pleasure, and the more joyous the reward in the fruits of his victim's imminent destruction.

But something different had happened with Dudley. Something of Dudley's own light had shone through his avatar and Rajapaksa had been pulled to it without realizing why. Things had proceeded much further than Rajapaksa could have ever thought possible. For Dudley's part, there was something of his brother's love, of his father's love, that came through the Tamil woman on the other side, the dark-skinned beauty who lived in Switzerland and modelled saris for a living. Without intending to, Dudley became more and more distant from his wife and children. He spent more and more time in front of the computer, conversing with the bold beauty on the other side of the dating interface. "If you don't like my sweets, why then do you visit my shop?" asked Rajapaksa coyly, echoing a line that his own wife had used on him a long time ago.

Well, one thing led to another; they broke lines that they had established for themselves, and the two brothers had cybersex. The experience was so shattering, tender, and profound, so unlike the real experiences that they'd had with their own wives, that each was prompted to finally, blushingly, drop his facade and reveal his true identity to the other. What shock! What horror! That's when Mahinda and Dudley Rajapaksa realized for the first time that they'd been committing digital incest!

The realization, so disturbing and shattering, had caused the two brothers to not talk to each other since that event. Coupled with the guilt from that dreadful event at Sigiriya rock so many years ago, Rajapaksa worried that his favourite brother might even take his own life.

But alas, the crown, heavy with responsibility, could not be removed forever. There were other things at hand. With the successful elimination of presidential term limits, Rajapaksa could now begin to relax during the Roman feast days – an endless line of Rajapaksa busts commemorating his hold on power would stretch down the future hallways of President's House.

To celebrate their successes, he had gotten the brothers, Gota, Basil, and Chamal, together for Saturnalian feasts at the Old Parliament Building. They cleared everyone out and women, except as slaves, were verboten. The brothers reclined on flat couches after having dipped in the caldarium. Slaves served them lavish courses of eggs, shellfish, stuffed dormice (which had to be imported from England), boiled meats, dove, roast boar, honey cakes, stuffed dates, fruit, and spiced loaves. The slaves would slice up the food and then fan the Rajapaksas with palm fronds so that the brothers would have to work as little as possible, saving their utmost energies for salivating, masticating, and digesting.

Mahinda eyed Basil and Chamal and observed that he could eat as much as they all could eat together. If they were stuck in an elevator with no recourse for food, Rajapaksa wondered which brother he would eat first. Basil was leathery and tall while Chamal was old and soft. Chamal would be the easiest to digest but Gota would probably be the juiciest, being small and round like an excitable grape. Was it strange to think like this – did his brothers ever wonder the same thing?

It had taken a while to find the stride of these bacchanals. In the early days, they had dressed as Pharaohs and briefly even toyed with performing Druidic rites. Now that the barbarians at the gates were quelled, the choice was clear. Rajapaksa snacked on a jackal's tongue and an overwhelming love for his family kindled and grew in his heart; the joy suffused him. He was a family man, a simple man. Even now, he'd give up the robin's eggs and all the spiced hyena spleens to have Shiranthi, his wife, beside him. They were not in love as they once had been, it was true, and she was considerably larger, but so was he. Her hair now looked like a porcupine's pelt. Three sons and two presidential terms later, it was difficult to snatch moments of time like he used to when they were newly wedded. He had tried to pull her onto his lap last week but she pushed herself off his knees and said, "Aii, what are you trying to do? I'm not a trapeze artist to be able to balance on so small a perch." When he had puckered his lips in displeasure, she continued with a shrewd smile: "Come, Mahinda, you're not the man you once were. Now, even your belly has a belly."

It was true – sometimes, in the middle of the night when he got up to use the loo, he had to grope down to find his penis. It was hidden between the folds of fat. Sometimes he could not tell where the fat on his thighs ended and the fat on his belly began. Groping around for his penis was as frustrating as trying to pull loose change out of a sofa in the dead of night, as his wife repeatedly reminded him. He had been shy when courting Shiranthi and his penis got semi-hard when he thought of her being crowned Miss Sri Lanka in 1973. O glorious moment! She was quite the radiant victor – she wore confidence and stature as if they were raiment over her tall frame – something Rajapaksa would not experience for himself until much later.

"Another dormouse, sir?" a slave offered him a plate. The syrupy sweetness of roasted dormice, heavy in the air, brought him back to the feast and he looked at the others gorging themselves. He gazed lovingly on his brother Basil who was Senior Presidential Advisor. It had been Basil's idea to have these bacchanals. Basil had always been the smartest of the Rajapaksas, an idea man, but sometimes his ideas would run away with him and Mahinda was left with the task of implementing their kernels while bringing Basil back to reality. For example, after reading an essay by Jonathan Swift, Basil suggested a program where bankrupt Tamils, livelihoods devastated by the war and with too many mouths to feed, could sell their littlest ones to the Singhalese who needed tender young flesh for stew and recipes. Calf was sometimes hard to come by but human calves were even more desirable. It was a win-win situation. No, no, no, Rajapaksa had to tell him, this was not something they could pass into legislation. For one thing, the Buddhists, who were largely vegetarian, would be offended at not being included in the process. And then, with these Roman feasts, Basil had wanted to not only role play the feasts but build an entire Roman villa with steam baths and heating system. He wanted the Tamils to wear iron collars around their necks to signify their slavery and to build a replica of Hadrian's wall to permanently keep the barbarians in the North and East at bay. Rajapaksa liked this idea better but once again, the Buddhists... he had to remember where his support was. It was true, said some, that with his large belly and genial smile, Rajapaksa looked somewhat like the Buddha himself – like a bodhisattva – all he needed was the long pierced earlobes and the ability to cross his legs, which was difficult as the belly inevitably got in the way.

At these times, despite the food and the excess, Rajapaksa became despondent and depressed. A strange mood descended upon him when he remembered his family, his parents and grandparents, his uncles, his sisters, who were not there in the room with him. At such times, it seemed as if the best people were absent. Dudley. His thoughts immediately turned sour and an angry flash, a taste like iron filings, filled his mouth. The worm ate the flower still. One could say that all the abductions, the official denials, the torture, and the oppression came from the anxiety this worm provoked upon his gut; he never knew when it would uncoil itself from underneath the sweetest dormouse and strike for the heart.

A low keening broke Rajapaksa out of his ever-descending reveries. The slaves looked over their shoulders to see two figures on the other side of the room lope in slowly, shadowy behind the steam rising from the caldarium. The two men were old for their gait was slow and they shuffled as if with great exertion; they were dressed in togas but wore the fabric wrapped around their heads as if hooded. The slaves immediately prepared two extra places at the feast. Rajapaksa was about to stop them but then the two unannounced visitors did an extraordinary thing. They changed direction and walked onto the steaming waters of the caldarium, came directly at Rajapaksa and his clan.

Without sinking, the two men immersed themselves in the scalding steam rising from the salty waters and made their way, now dissembling, then reappearing, across the surface of the pool. As they came closer, Rajapaksa realized that they weren't wearing togas at all but sarongs. And those weren't hoods over their faces – where there were supposed to be faces were simply a few strands of hair, the curve of noses, the barest outlines of lips. One wore a shawl around his neck which Rajapaksa had mistaken for the fold of the toga over the shoulder and as he looked closer, the shawl seemed to remind him of his own. If not for the fact that both figures were a chalky, powdery white, he would have said that he was looking at himself and Gota floating into view before them.

One of the figures – the one with the shawl – bent down and tried to pick up a quail's egg with difficulty. He tried for a while to raise it to his lips, then let it fall reluctantly. The figure then slumped down in despair into one of the spaces created for them. The other patted his companion good-naturedly on the shoulder and then sat down himself.

The slaves and the soothsayer, not to mention the other brothers, had become greatly agitated. One of the slaves began muttering "Adai! Adai!" and slapping his forehead with great agitation. Rajapaksa hissed at him and then drawing himself up imperiously, dismissed them all except for his brothers and the soothsayer.

The ghostly figures continued to try and pick up items, as if unfamiliar with them, testing them in their hands like children, but incapable of drawing the token strength that even a baby possesses, failing in their task. The one without a shawl could make a peacock feather flutter briefly but this was the sum of his accomplishments.

"Who are you?" cried Rajapaksa, "Evil spirits, why do you disturb our feast?"

"Pipe down, pipe down," said the one who had rustled the peacock feather. His voice was like the wind blowing through a hollow bone. "Don't you recognize who I am, boy? I leave you for a little while and you begin to put on airs."

"Father?" cried Rajapaksa, unbelievingly. "Can it be? Merciful Buddha, has he sent you back to us?"

"Alright, alright," said the ghostly figure, "don't make a fuss." Then turning to the traveller beside him, "He was always such a baby, you know."

Rajapaksa looked to his right and now recognized the abstract figure of his uncle, D. M., the Lion of Ruhuna, whom people said he resembled, and whose shawl Rajapaksa had adopted as his own. Words left him and sobs choked his chest. With great excitement, he threw his arms around the two figures to embrace them but he moved too fast and clutched smoke. He fell forward on his belly. The disturbed forms broke and resettled like particles of ash in emulsion and the smell was quite horrid; Rajapaksa felt as if a cat had drowned and then its wet remains had been smeared into paste.

Coughing, fanning the air around him, Rajapaksa finally stammered, "Why have you come to us now? Is something important going to happen in the future?" (and then, daring to voice his most secret dream), "Will I, will I, finally be crowned emperor in my lifetime?"

"Settle down, boy," said the shade of his father, trying to blow on the peacock feather again without success. "A parliamentary seat was good enough in my day..."

"...look how greedy the next generation becomes!" finished uncle D. M.

"Did you also come here with a message for your children?" Chamal asked their uncle, now having recovered his senses and remembering that he was the eldest of the brothers.

"No, no..." replied D. M.

"He was just bored and decided to come with me," said their father. "I told him one day 'I'm going to take a trip to see my boys.' "

"And you didn't want to take Ma?" asked Basil, "How is Ma? Is she well?" Basil had always clung a little too hard to their mother.

"Well, boy," said their father, ghostly lips twisting to a scowl, "that woman's gone and done something. Boys, do you know what your mother's done? She's gone and stolen something valuable from me."

"What is it, thatha?" asked Chamal.

"Your mother's gone and run away, boys. She's stolen herself away from me! She's left me desolate!"

D. M. agreed with his brother and the boys said nothing, feeling foolish in their togas and surrounded by such repast. They remembered their father's theories of how women were like land and that an unplowed woman was no better than unplowed land. These speeches of his had made them quite uncomfortable as children and they worried that he was going to launch into one now. Instead, the shade of D. A. simply continued his paltering attempts to blow on the peacock feather.

"Dad, will you stop blowing on that feather and look at me?" Rajapaksa broke down after a while. He had not been accustomed to people ignoring him as of late; it provoked in him a great agitation.

"Boy, don't you raise your tone with me..." clucked his father with displeasure.

"You remember who he is," said D. M. "He brought you into this world and..."

"I can take you out of it, quite literally," continued his father. "You're not too young for me to take over my knee, you know. Come here!"

"What?" stammered Rajapaksa.

"I said *come here*, boy!" The smoky finger of his father unequivocally pointed towards his ghostly lap. "Don't make me have to ask you again."

Rajapaksa felt all his years, his newfound cloak of power and authority, drain from him along with the blood in his cheeks. He had not felt this vague terror, the bottom drop out of his heart, since he was a child. With a lost look in his eyes, he stirred and obeyed. With faltering steps, he went over to his ghostly father's knee and attempted to bend over it. There was no stable form, no weight to support him. Rajapaksa had to use his own knees and feet, tucked under his haunches, to keep from falling over. His belly wobbled with the strain and effort. The pain of keeping him balanced thus and the humiliation of being disciplined in front of his brothers, his inferiors, was worse than any physical effect his father's ghostly hand could have. The ectoplasmic hand, if it could be felt at all on his padded posterior, tickled rather than hurt. He thought of a similar time when his father had tried to spank him as an adult for mixing up the words *ontology* and *oncology* on a university application and ending up in the wrong program.

"Well... well...," puffed his father, wheezing in ghostly breaths, "Maybe this will teach you a proper lesson."

"Actually, we were supposed to get here two weeks ago," said D. M.

"But we got sidetracked," added their father, "We followed the cricket team around for a while."

"And we were able to go into women's changing rooms in department stores without being seen," elaborated D. M.

"You don't need to tell them details!" hissed their father.

"So why exactly are you here?" asked Gota after a while.

"Mostly because of you, genius!" scolded their father. Gota, flighty and excitable Gota, had always received the brunt of their father's distempers and foul moods as a child. Gota was an irrepressible rough peg that D. A. constantly tried to sand down. In the end, Gota had sworn off politics, joined the army and after a frustrating career fighting earlier cadres of the LTTE, moved to the States to work in computers. When his family had asked him why, Gota had replied that computers weren't unreasonable and never let you down. Now, despite his prominence and power, he felt all his status and victory stripped from him merely by the spectral presence of his father and uncle, the threat of a ghostly beating, and the recrimination in their voices.

"What do you mean?" asked Gota, unable to eradicate the hint of a boy's whimper.

"You and your brothers have done such a good job," hissed their father.

"That the afterlife is overflowing with Tamils," concluded their uncle.

"We can't turn our heads in any direction without some darkie leering at us!"

The two spectres traded sentences as if speaking with one mind. Rajapaksa sensed that death gave them some extrasensory access to each other's thoughts. He wondered if he and his brothers might also share access to one another's thoughts in the afterlife, once they were finally dead and buried. Some super-Rajapaksa? Images of himself and Dudley suddenly rose in the back of his mind and he had to shake himself to get the nausea and iron filings out of his mouth. He distracted himself by wondering if there were any dinosaurs in heaven; he had always wanted to meet a dinosaur – a stegosaurus or a T-rex preferably – but he sensed that this was not the best time to ask. If they could reanimate dinosaurs in the future, like in *Jurassic Park*, then they could probably reanimate Rajapaksa and, perhaps, he would never have to die. The ghosts of his father and uncle brought Rajapaksa's mind back to the topic at hand.

"They're cracking their coconuts in the street, they wear their sarongs with no banians, and they turn up the volume of their Tamil music without any heed to what other people say. It's not fair!" stated D. M.

"All because of you lot! You've given them their Eelam, only it's in the damned afterlife! And now, since they're dead, we can't do anything to them so don't try to advise us with your usual tactics," stated their father, stumping Rajapaksa who was desperately trying to come up with a rejoinder.

"In fact, it's the opposite of here!" cried their uncle. "They're the majority and we're the minority. They impose restrictions, tell us what we can and can not do, and populate our neighbourhoods in heaven."

"So, for me, if not for anybody else, could you and your brothers give it a bloody rest? For all of us, I'm begging you! Just take your spoils and enjoy yourselves. Or if you're feeling like you actually want to do something, remedy a little. A bit of redress and reparation wouldn't hurt."

"After all, we didn't tell you to go kill them *all*," added their uncle, cocking his head.

The Rajapaksa brothers looked at each other with mouths open. Never in a million years did they expect their father and uncle to return in this fashion, with these words. They had thought that they did what they did in memory of their forefathers. They were redressing the petty losses and bitter disappointments endured by their father, his loss of seat and ill health before an untimely death. To see him, as alive and ill-tempered as ever, snatched the joy of victory from their hands and left a taste of ashes in their mouths. They looked at the feast before them and did not want to eat any more. Soon, they would have to take a trip to the vomitorium to purge the day's feasting and then have the slaves tidy things for the next day, but they would not have the same sense of stuffed satiation and gorged appetite they normally could rely on to get them through a week's tedium of meetings and conferences.

"Tell us more," said Chamal, wearily.

"Well, the darkies have elected a supreme leader," said their father, casting his hollow eyes around the gathering.

"Guess who it is!" chuckled their uncle.

"Oh no!"

"Oh yes! That's right, geniuses!" scowled their father, "It's everybody's favourite sharp dresser — that idiot Prabhakaran! I swear that man has more lives than a damned cat!"

"You can't be serious," exclaimed Gota, feeling all of his work undone.

"And not just that," continued their uncle, "he's worse than you boys. A real martinet! He makes us change our clothes at least twice a day! He orders us to make our beds and cook our own meals. He's a real stickler for cleanliness. A real power trip, that man!"

"Can't you do anything? Revolt?" asked Basil.

"No, everything's on the up and up – it's the afterlife, you know, he was elected cleanly there," said D. M. "All we can do is leave for a while."

"We're going to travel around a little bit," sighed their father. "I always said that I'd take Dudley to Disney World when he was a boy... and I never had any time while I was alive. That's the way these things are. Do you have any money?"

"What?!"

"Do you have any money?" asked their father again. "I want to take Dudley on Space Mountain and I don't have any money. They take all yours away when you enter nirvana. And properly speaking, they don't know that we're gone so..."

"...and we want to see Michael Jackson's grave," concluded their uncle. "He was a gifted yet troubled young man."

"Do you want us to give any special message to your brother Dudley?" inquired their father, looking up.

"No..." stammered Rajapaksa.

"Well, maybe we can take a quick look at your brother now – " D. A. snapped his fingers and pointed towards the soothsayer. "Let's see something."

The soothsayer was simply an out-of-work actor and bided his time at these gatherings looking grim. Suddenly, the incense and camphor in his urn came to life and gurgled. The smoke and mists rose all around them, the fog and vapours filling the room so that the brothers started to choke and cough. The smoke and the spices poured into their lungs, tears came to their eyes, their nostrils could hardly function.

Their eyes became accustomed to the smoke and the grainy surroundings so that they could see whispery, phantasmagoric images raise themselves in the air, flicker, then disappear before others took their place. First, they saw Prabhakaran, overlord and master of the afterworld, marshaling Singhalese and Tamils alike. Everyone looked pious and serious. All their clothes were starchily pressed and clean. It was like an inverse of the Victory parade that Rajapaksa had recently overseen on the Galle Face. Prabhakaran turned around from the afterworld and smiled his large Tiger's grin at the brothers, flashing his teeth. There was no moustache! Prabhakaran was denuded of his moustache! For some reason, this enraged Rajapaksa more than anything else as he had always been envious of Prabhakaran's mighty, nervy, flowing moustache – it seemed as resolute and intense as the mighty commander himself – whereas Rajapaksa's moustache had been compared to two caterpillars going about the slow business of mating. *My business is to adorn this famous face*, Prabhakaran's moustache had seemed to say, *I will carry out my mission with the utmost follicular dedication.* Nothing made Rajapaksa sadder than to see it permanently effaced from the cheek and jowl of the grinning supreme commander. *So it's final then?* wondered Rajapaksa. *You rule the afterlife without a moustache – and do you also have dominion over the stegosauruses and T-rexes? Do you also count them amongst your subjects?*

The wisps of smoke blew around to reveal an image of Rajapaksa as a younger man, clear-skinned and idealistic. His belly had shrunk back to a respectable pot. He waited for the beautiful woman who wore confidence and stature as raiment over her tall frame. He stood backstage with a bouquet of roses for Shiranthi while she finished up an appearance at some cultural show or other. Finally, the beauty queen came backstage and Rajapaksa presented her with the flowers.

"I have enough flowers, when are you going to ask me to marry you?" asked Shiranthi, peeved. "When are you going to tell your mother? I've already told my father, the Commodore."

"We're still getting to know each other, why are you rushing me?" complained Rajapaksa.

"If you don't like my sweets, why then do you frequent my shop?" scowled his future wife, applying a fresh coat of cherry lipstick to her lips. She stretched her mouth open and then looked in the mirror, not deigning to look at Rajapaksa directly. Shiranthi dabbed the excess lipstick with a napkin and eyed the squirming young man with the vague, indecisive moustache, daring him to make a move.

He obviously could not.

Shiranthi had to turn around and pull Rajapaksa towards her and pick up his hands, forcing them to lie upon and cover her breasts which heaved through her sari.

An image of their brother Dudley, in front of his computer with a drink in his hand, weeping over the keyboard, flitted past.

The brothers became attentive, puzzled. They knew their brother to be a gentle, agreeable sort. He was well-off and happily married, a long way away from the tribulations and operatic struggles heaving across Sri Lanka. They had not heard of any accidents or emergencies that would give cause to such an outpouring of grief.

Then the image of Rajapaksa playing with himself, wetting a finger with spittle and tracing it around the soft erogenous zones of his own nipples, in front of his own laptop. The famous one which he could not be separated from.

Chamal, being the eldest, was the first to realize what was going on. The text from the two computer screens and their IM boxes flashed past. All four brothers and their ghostly father and uncle watched in amazement as the strange mating ritual between brother and brother unfolded in cyberspace. Their jaws dropped open as they saw the acts of digital love come to their unnatural end and the fallout. The reconnection, then the ultimate sundering of the thin wire mesh which strung over the ocean, between two brothers, separated by history and time.

The phantasmagoric images swung to the past to see all the brothers as young boys, children on an excursion to Sigiriya rock. Their father was absent and the boys were both pleased and anxious at his long remove. The sweetness, freedom, and daring which hung in the air. Inevitably, it turned into fear and shame as the day's events progressed and the priest entered the picture. For shame, the adult brothers hung their heads in agony to see and understand where things were with Dudley, noble Dudley, keeper of the flame. They all felt disgusted and sick. They felt the food upon which they had gorged themselves, the quail eggs and dormice, come up and threaten to burn their esophaguses.

Their father and uncle sputtered and gasped, for once wordless. Not knowing what else to do, D. A., aware of the limits of his own incorporeality, ordered Gota to beat Rajapaksa. Then he ordered Rajapaksa to spank Gota. Not to leave the job half done, D. A. ordered Chamal to spank Basil and Basil to spank Chamal. The boys, filled with shame, obeyed without protestation. Despondently, they shuffled forward and bent over, rendering up their toga-clad posteriors and enduring their beatings with half-hearted sobs.

At some point during the beatings, the shades disappeared. They took their vague and drowsy forms back to the realm they had come from. The boys repaired to the vomitorium where they expurgated the food and the memories of what they'd seen and done. When they had finished, their heads hurt and it was as if their entire intestines were writhing, spilt and bloody on the floor. Something tied them beyond wealth, beyond success, beyond mere power itself. It was shame. Shame for the excess, shame for the knowledge, shame for the loss of innocence of their one good brother who, though remote and inconsequential, had once redeemed them with his honesty and goodness. Now, Rajapaksa's defilement was also their own. It felt as if with Dudley's corruption, the last vestige of possibility of redemption was also gone. They looked at each other, looked at the mists from the caldarium and the incense around them, looked beyond the line of death at the vanished presences of their father and uncle, and felt a shiver. It was the end, the decline of everything they had built and mounted, the cracks and fault lines in their civilization. It was the end of them and their empire, their presence upon the earth and their importance. It was as if they were nothing more than wisps of smoke disappearing into the ground.

Thosai

ATTENTION: This is not Ma Rajapaksa speaking but a group of freedom fighters. There has been too much emphasis placed on Singhalese dishes in this book and not enough Tamil content. Therefore, we are hijacking this recipe and substituting a Tamil dish. Don't call it 'terrorism' unless you are terrified by delicious Dravidian cuisine! Thosais are a treat to look forward to on weekends and you can improvise by adding bay leaves or other garnishes of your own choosing into the mix. Enjoy!

Ingredients:
1 cup Urad dahl
½ cup of raw rice
½ teaspoon of pepper
¼ teaspoon of fenugreek
2 tablespoons of ghee
1 red onion
3 dried chilies broken down
a few curry leaves
salt (to taste)
½ teaspoon of cumin

Wash and soak your dahl, rice, and fenugreek. Grind these three into a smooth paste and mix them well together. Once they have become a smooth paste, cover it and leave it overnight. In the morning, add water to it and mix it all into a thick batter. Leave this aside and in a small pan, heat the ghee, adding in the onions and dried chilies. Finally, add the curry leaves. Cook this mixture until it is golden brown and then add the cooked mixture to your original batter. Mix in the ground salt, pepper, and cumin. Next, heat up an iron griddle or cast-iron pan and rub its surface with oil to make it smooth. Taking a ladle full of batter, pour it onto the surface of the pan and smooth it flat with the back of your ladle or spoon. Once the colour is golden brown, turn it over onto the other side (without breaking) and cook for a few minutes.

You can enjoy this with seeni sambol or coconut sambol or, if you want, paruppu (although that's a little boring). Now, eat, eat, don't let the food get cold. Is that all you're going to have? Come on; eat more so that you can work hard to liberate our people!

Sincerely,

Terrroristz

(the Terrorists)

The Secret Story

Congratulations on making it this far through the book. As a reward for your loyal readership, we have provided a hidden story, somewhat like a hidden track on a CD. There will be some who say that this story should not have been included, that it extenuates and breaks even the extreme limits of taste and decorum that have been hitherto flirted with. Before you join their ranks, think upon the pickpockets and poachers you have elected to do their murderous work in the world and the reluctance most people feel to lift a finger or whisper a word against them.

Even now, somewhere in the world, bombs are being dropped upon hospitals. Somewhere, women are being raped while others have their unborn children ripped from their stomachs. Men are being tortured and detained not so much for the information they might hold but to emphasize the rule of force. Children are learning the specifications of which calibre bullets are to be used with which rifles. Their parents are familiar with the practical ins and outs of priming detonation devices. This has happened countless times before and will happen countless times again.

So, before you go wagging your prudish fingers at us, think of the difference in scale of the relative crimes before you. On the one hand, you have the hot bang and bluster of a few stories, 'a tale told by an idiot, full of sound and fury, signifying nothing.' On the other, the cool and detached termination of hundreds of thousands of lives. The carpet bombing of whole countries, the wholesale shattering of lives, the ruination of families. The implosion of an ancient culture within a hot parched afternoon.

Our tale does not have a date except to say that it is sadly set near the present day. If the story has numerous detractors and a great many faults, it at least possesses the virtue of brevity. It begins with Shiranthi Rajapaksa whom we have met but not really gotten to know. The first lady has been married to Mahinda Rajapaksa for a long time. She has come a long way from the plump beauty queen experiencing her cheery incursions into sports. Being the only girl in a family with two brothers, ruled by the stern patrician hand of their father, the Commodore Wickramasinghe, Shiranthi was used to having to put up with men and their inconstancy. But all her illustrious experience and achievement could not prepare her for what the future held.

As a young girl, she had thought that whomever she married must have the proud and noble bearing of her father. He shone in his navy lapels and pressed white suit. How decisive and commanding he had been, orchestrating and ordaining every aspect of his children's lives! Her brothers could not bear the old Commodore's authority but Shiranthi had felt reassured by it. Some of her fondest memories had been as a child accompanying the old Commodore. They were ferried to the warships that awaited inspection. She loved the feeling of being on the water which sparkled opal with amethyst glints. It seemed vast and lively in its infinite glory. As a little girl, she felt the rocking of the small skiff through her bones as they passed through the harbour. Her torso seemed to slide away from her pelvis, only to be brought back together at the last moment. Again and again. The skiff ferrying them out to the warships was a watery crèche. She was at the mercy of the world, at the mercy of absolute authority, something even stronger than her father. The Commodore seemed to understand this without words, the absolute exquisiteness of law and order upon that one thing which man had not one whit of power upon: the sea. How delicious the presumption to propose order upon so chaotic a territory!

In rare moments together, he would row his daughter out to sea himself until they were almost out of sight of land. They were so fragile, so infinitesimal, rocking upon the watery welkin of sea, beneath the rollicking clouds, above the scudding waves. Father and daughter grew close in those moments, bonded by powerlessness in the midst of nature's terrible might and beauty. Slowly, slowly, he would take them back to land and Shiranthi would have to collect and assemble herself, her small identity and burgeoning place in the world. The duties and the parts.

Mahinda had not been a sea man, in fact, knew nothing of the navy. Her father had initially approved because he was a lawyer then and there was no indication that Mahinda would ever become a politician. Rajapaksa had been favoured not so much because he impressed the old Commodore but because his horoscope was the only one Shiranthi's could be matched with.

The old Commodore put much more faith in the stars, which had guided sailors since time immemorial, than he did in politicians. If the Commodore had been given liberty to run things, the Sri Lankan Navy would simply have sailed up the coast and bombed the insurgent malcontents into submission. Their red earth would have been so broken up and silty, it would have simply crumbled and floated away. Thus would they have avoided all that nonsense in the eighties.

"We'll set their Eelam adrift, the landlubbers!" the Commodore rubbed his white-gloved hands together, "And then harpoon any survivors!

"That'll teach them the value of law and authority!" he offered gleefully. Visitors would simply smile and lift their teacups to their lips, not knowing what to say.

When Shiranthi or one of the boys had been naughty, the Commodore would mete out punishment by placing them under court martial. He read their accounts from the log, then assigned a sentence to be served in the 'hold'. The 'hold' was a heavy teak almirah which was locked from the outside. While the culprit was locked in its dark confines, the others in the family rocked the almirah to and fro as if it were a coffin upon the watery seas. Her brothers always came out panting and terrified, clutching their throats. Their shirts were soaked, with hair salty and eyes that rolled back in their heads in terror. But Shiranthi sort of liked it. She saw her time in the hold as part of a game played with her father, a secret between the two of them. In its absence of light and sound, the smell of wood and dust, the almirah was like an old skiff upon the sea. She felt the motion of its sway in space, her torso sliding away from her pelvis and then coming back together at the last moment, the sense of darkness and abstraction a welcome reprieve from the sense of time.

Now, time marched on and the only reminder of those bountiful and freshly healthy days was her second son, Yoshitha. He owned the Carlton Sports Network and had joined the Navy in honour of the old Commodore. When this favourite son had asked about the circumstances of his birth, Shiranthi naturally lied.

Lying came easily to her now and she lied to all her sons and others close to her; sometimes she felt that lying was the most natural and primitively strong way for a woman to maintain sound relations with those around her, especially in this cruel and wicked world where to do bad was often thought good and to do good was accounted as folly. There was something watery and easy about lying. The easy way the truth slipped beneath the waves of the day to day. She had told Yoshitha that Mahinda and she had conceived while having accepted an invitation to stay at a villa on the island of Taprobane near Weligama Bay.

The truth was that her husband had seized her one day in an uncharacteristic moment of lust. Shiranthi had returned from a trip to Singapore and had come back with the latest fashions, among them leather jackets, tight jeans, leg warmers, large golden hoop earrings, and a woman's set of leather pants and jacket in a tiger print. It was the late eighties and no one knew any better. She had worn the last two items, the tiger-print pants and jacket with the leather fringe, along with the hoop earrings, and was admiring herself in the mirror. Her husband, Mahinda, walked in and she saw his reflection in the corner of the mirror. His head rubbernecked and his eyes started out of his head. Mahinda jumped up on her from behind, violently pressing his thighs against her pelvis and digging his fingers into her sides. She had had to carry him, stumbling to the bed in a sort of piggyback ride, where Mahinda insisted on taking her from behind, slavishly panting as if he had not eaten for weeks. Shiranthi had wanted to take her clothes off but her husband had insisted she keep them on, lowering her pants only a little, and dug at her like a pneumatic drill, slobbering wet saliva against the back of her neck. In seconds, it was over. A moment of surprising pleasure and nine months of relative pain. Yoshitha had been a large and healthy baby swimming in the waves of her amniotic tide.

As Yoshitha grew, he reminded his mother of the old Commodore. There was some satisfaction in that. Her life was now a far cry from those early days when the Commodore began his inspections with a twelve-gun salute and marshaled the children's lives into an exacting (and exciting) routine: breakfast, exercise, studies, sports, piano, prayers, and so forth. If any of his family strayed from their timetables, they would be placed in the hold.

Her capability for ardour and physical love diminished as Yoshitha grew up, ripened, and left. Her third and final son, Rohitha, was an egghead and strange, at turns charming and moody. He was as different from Yoshitha as the sky is from the sea. And like the sky, his ambition and intellect seemed limitless as he pursued a cutting path through the sciences, medicine, and astronomy. Whence came all this intelligence? Surely not from her or Mahinda!

She and Mahinda possessed large appetites and their separation grew in girth as did their waistlines. She matched him pound for pound, jowl for jowl, and that was all that linked them now. Their distant love was like a fragile thread hanging over some monsooned sea. Now, if he were to try and make love to her, it would take near half an hour to find his penis and pull it out from the mess between his belly and his thighs. Another half an hour to get it straight and erect. It was like watching someone pulling change out from the folds of a couch. Very sad. In public, of course, she deferred to her husband, playing the meek and perfect hostess. Inside, she seethed with curses and contempt.

Her frustrations had to do as much with her own failings as those foisted on her by Mahinda. Whereas once she had been fresh and healthy, a beauty queen and sports aficionado, she was now a kept woman, a war queen. It was not so bad except for the physical toll it took on her body. The constant smiling and hypocrisy! The knowledge that her husband was nothing like the strict and disciplined father who had now succumbed to death, the sea of eternity. Her flesh seemed to accrue mass with the wealth that rose in the Rajapaksas' coffers. With each new level of power, responsibility, and entitlement, a new line appeared on her face, drawing her skin like cheesecloth into a scarred net of crow's feet and scabby pores. Her hair, once lustrous and shiny, became a porcupine's pelt. Where once she had seemed lovely and sweet, her visage was now marked by a wicked grin, a salacious smile. It was like the portrait of Dorian Gray, except that Mahinda was Dorian, his face smooth and baby-like, while she became his canvas. She continued to wither and age with each new horror he perpetrated upon the country and its people.

Shiranthi had tried in the early years of his presidency to deal with the growing distance between them by looking for lovers. However, with such a high profile, taking a lover and keeping things secret were two different things. Sri Lanka was a small island and news travelled fast; in matters of state, the country pretended to be modern but in reality, all of the old ways and values still held. Furthermore, it did not help her love life that she had aged and lost her looks.

One of the captured Tamils (the 'darkies' as Mahinda fondly referred to them), was brought in to be a temporary slave in their household while Shiranthi looked for a new cook. This boy, at the most twenty, with no more than ten hairs on his chin, had worked in a restaurant before being inducted into the war and knew his way around Singhalese dishes. He made an excellent thosai and a delectable seeni sambol to go with it. His arms were sinewy and the skinny yet tight muscles exerted themselves like darting fish as he chopped onions and pressed cumin leaves and crushed turmeric.

"What pressure those hands could exert upon my skin..." she idly commented, standing in the doorway to the kitchen.

The Tamil boy looked up. He was surprised at being talked to or even acknowledged. Usually, he cooked the food, cleared away the dishes, swept the floors, and then retired to a pallet of straw that lay in the basement. He looked at this porpoise in her sari, moon-eyed and chirping at him, her blubber bursting out at the folds at her sides. She rocked her hips but he did not understand what she was saying. He did not much care. Frankly, he was sick of this enforced servitude; fighting in the war had been less frightful and less hostile. It was the maid's day off. Guards were posted outside the house but could not enter. Yet there were greater dangers inside the house than out.

The young slave allowed himself to be seduced, thinking it might mean a chance at freedom, and found himself being danced, almost carried, by the first lady to the bedchamber.

Mahinda stopped in to pick up some files he forgot at home while his driver idled in the car. The president heard the noises coming from the bedroom. He followed the sighs and moans, wondering what on earth was going on, only to find his wife naked, between the royal sheets with the high thread count that they had bought, pressing herself onto their darkie slave. Rajapaksa immediately went into a rage and sprang forward.

"You have seen the queen naked!" he roared. He wished to tear out the insolent boy's throat! Instead, he grabbed a pillow and jumped onto the boy, pressing his knees against the darkie's chest, so that the boy could not move, and then smothered the boy with the pillow. The once privileged cook struggled, his skinny fishlike arms flopping all over the place. It was all in vain. He muttered something in Tamil into the pillow that sounded like "Amma" and then ceased to struggle. The pillow ripped under Rajapaksa's fury and goose feathers floated in the air.

Mahinda knelt there panting. His wife slowly put her underwear on and then calmed her husband down, fetching him a glass of water. Already, she could feel the crow's feet receding across her face, scuttling into the bone, the battle lines and faults pulling themselves back into her flesh. While her husband panted, she realized why he, the most meek and timid of men in comparison to her father, a man who could barely make love to her once he had her, enjoyed battle so much. It was absolutely invigorating! It was absolute joy! It took years from the bones and pumped oxygen through the blood!

They played out the same scenario many times over the intervening years. Mahinda and she never talked about it, nor did they ever make direct plans. The brutal pantomime became a substitute for sex. And sometimes, rarely, a prelude to sex. They called it *Candaules and Gyges* after the tale in Herodotus. Shiranthi would seduce a man, usually a Tamil worker who had no family and would not be missed, taking him as far as the bedchamber where she disrobed. Perhaps seduction was too loose a word. She coerced him. She cajoled him. And in her own way, she enticed him. Mahinda would wait behind the door with an ancient mace like Gyges and then at the appropriate moment, would jump out and cry, "You have seen the queen naked!" and club the poor victim to death. The man in question would not even have time to raise his hands to his face. The sheets were instantly sprayed with blood. The two lay there panting afterwards in the warm mist of their climax. Blood and feathers floated upon the air.

And this was how their third son was born. Rohitha could have been a joy but there was something different about him – with his long shaggy Western hair and guitar, he looked like a hippie from the seventies. Yet, despite the youthful insolence and surfer attitude, he was involved with designing a satellite with the Chinese. Shiranthi didn't quite understand it. She came to his room and saw all his clothes strewn about the floor. He sat in the middle of them, munching on hot mix and playing his Nintendo DS. The maid had only cleaned yesterday! How could he make such a mess so fast? Did the youngster not realize what a pig he was?

Shiranthi pulled a nice silk shirt from under the boy to stop it from being ruined but he ignored her, hardly batted an eye. He just continued playing with his video game: racing cars or shooting people or whatever it was. The controller jumped in his hand and electronic beeps and whistles issued from the TV. She left him, closing the door gently, and looked at the pearl silk shirt in her hand. There was a time when such an item would have been a great rarity and no one could dare treat clothes thus. An oil stain covered the front of the shirt and she knew enough to know that it could not be washed by throwing it into a machine or beating it against some rock. She placed some spittle on her fingernail and rubbed it into the oil and tried to knead out the stain. "Out, damn spot!" she spat in futile curse as she made her way to her own room, her private room away from Mahinda, her sanctum sanctorum.

She still spent her nights with Mahinda in their bed although they hardly touched anymore, did not even come close. They had stopped playing *Candaules and Gyges* a long time ago. Mahinda was busy now; half the time she did not even know where his work took him. She had had to make her own arrangements to continue the sports that now consumed her life, that now rejuvenated her. It was a pity. No longer the volleyball net, the field hockey stick, for this little one. There was a time to put away playthings and that time was now long past. She rejuvenated herself according to an old tradition, an old recipe that not even Rajapaksa's mother had known about.

Shiranthi put Rohitha's shirt into a laundry hamper and then peeled off her own clothes and deposited them there also. Slowly, with grim and deliberate satisfaction, she donned a bathrobe and nothing else. The tacit understanding between herself and Mahinda had now moved far beyond bedroom games like *Candaules and Gyges*. He played his games to stay young and she played hers. He acknowledged her needs and tacitly gave her the means and funds to carry them out although she could tell he was disgusted.

What did it matter? They were beyond such petty considerations now. All that mattered was the slowing of time, the halting of age, to lock the door and turn away the reaper as much as it was in her power to do so. By whatever means necessary. *Come, you spirits*, she thought to herself as she walked through the bathroom which had been prepped and left for her sole use, *stop up the access and passage to time*.

Inside the bathroom, from the oversized ceiling above the bath, hung butcher's hooks with the corpses of fresh bodies pinned to them. Each hook hoisted a recently impaled young Tamil man and Tamil woman. Seven and seven in total. Virgins all. Paid as tribute from various villages, the virgins arrived on a monthly cycle, in time for the new moon. She cut her thigh with an obsidian knife that lay nearby for this purpose. The tributes' virgin blood dripped down into the tub and joined hers in a warm and sizzling coagulation of fluids.

Shiranthi voiced the rest of the ancient invocation and shed her bathrobe, climbed slowly into the tub. The first step was always the hardest and she dallied, letting the blood seep between her toes and cover her thigh with its dark viscosity. Slowly, she slid into the blood that covered her entire body, trying to pour in at her orifices with its warmth and youth. It felt thick and sturdy, rocking her to and fro with its waves. The red mist rose and fell back as she allowed herself to be submerged, her torso sliding away from her pelvis and then rejoining at the last possible moment. It was something like being upon the sea.

She stopped up the access to remorse and imagined the crow's feet and lines pulling themselves back into her skin, the battle lines of her face being redrawn, boundaries erasing and distinctions melting.

For the next hour, she was not to be disturbed and felt at peace with the world.

Carrot Sambal

Well, of all the nerve! Get your own book, you damn terrorists! Is one not safe from terrorism even after one is dead? We're going to get back on track now with a simple and quick dish that can be used to garnish a variety of meals or serve as complement to the standard rice and curries.

Ingredients:
3 medium carrots finely grated
¼ cup of grated coconut
3 finely chopped shallots
2 finely chopped green chilies
salt (to taste)
the juice from ½ a lime

Simply mix all the ingredients together and then squeeze the lime on top. Enjoy, and make sure the terrorists don't steal your food.

Mahinda travels in the next story and employs his skills of diplomacy and subterfuge. A long time ago, I told him that his face was like a refrigerator where everyone could see its contents. I schooled him to be as sweet as jaggery on the outside while burning hot as chilies on the inside.

Big Trouble in Little Eelam

Rajapaksa and Gota fussed with their disguises in front of the mirror at the airport bathroom. Rajapaksa had shorn his head and wore a bright orange robe to look like a Buddhist monk. He had asked for a disguise that made him look like Caine from *Kung Fu* but the robe reminded him of the time he had worked on *The Dream of Dharmapala* – how easier things had been then when he simply wanted to be a cinematic heartthrob and dramatic genius! Instead, he had become another kind of star, the leading actor in the new exciting drama known as *Sri Lanka's Wars, Part IV: A New Hope!* The progression of states and epochs in the island's bloody history were like lives lived, each phase as different from the other as if the island itself were going through reincarnations until it shook off its dire karma and emerged into the light of a brand new nirvana. A light that he, Rajapaksa, would usher in as its crowning Buddha.

Gota was dressed like Tupac Shakur. Rajapaksa sighed. What was wrong with his younger brother? He suspected it was nothing that medication could not fix. Even his ghostly father's spanking had not done the trick. If anything, Gota had become even more moody and sullen since that time, as if the spanking from the ghost of their father had reverted him to a sullen teenager, a child. He withdrew into his inner sanctum for hours on end or fed his sharks at his home compound and would entertain no visitors. Indeed, the ministers were hesitant to visit him there as he and his wife fed their 'children' slabs of raw meat which were eagerly consumed amongst rows and rows of teeth while a litany of swear words and four-letter rants emitted from the living room speakers: Puff Daddy, Mase, Biggie Smalls, and of course, Gota's favourite, 2Pac.

In fact, Gota was wearing a 2Pac t-shirt right now with 'Thug Life' written on it, a yellow FUBU jacket, a Phillies baseball cap, retro Air Jordans, and Beats by Dr. Dre headphones. Rajapaksa and Gota were dressed incognito and travelling passenger class, like peasants, to Scarborough. Scarborough was part of the Greater Toronto Area, the de facto capital of Canada, and was said to hold the greatest concentration of Sri Lankan Tamils outside Sri Lanka. It burned his pride that so many Tamils had escaped the scourge that he and the other Rajapaksas had visited on their country. Somehow, these bastards had survived and thrived, only amassing their hordes and secret fortunes so they could continue their wicked terrorist ways in the New World. Not if Rajapaksa could help it!

It was Basil, the idea man, who had come up with the idea for this trip. Rajapaksa had been morose of late with no outlet for his mighty and imperious energies. Tourism was booming in Sri Lanka. The country's star was rising in the pan-Asian basin. They had finally fired that troublesome woman editor at *The Sunday Leader*. The future looked as cloudless as Colombo's bright skies. It would take Detective Columbo himself to discover the buried skeletons in Colombo's history! Rajapaksa's poor wife bore the brunt of his excess energy but she gave as good as she got.

Canada was a peace-loving and unsuspecting country. Like a fat turtle, it might be just the place a ferocious and ravenous lion such as himself could find his next meal. So he and Gota were off to Scarborough or 'Little Eelam' as they liked to call it. Without a worthy opponent like Prabhakaran to sharpen his claws against, Rajapaksa worried that his considerable energies would decay and founder. A scouting mission was just what was called for.

They would go to Little Eelam and see what was what. With any luck, this time next year, a host of Chengdu J-7 fighter planes, on loan from Hu Jintao and the Chinese, would be carpet bombing the Scarborough Town Centre.

"Do you have the passports, brother?" asked Gota, making sure his untucked t-shirt was just perfect.

"You must call me Field Commander Rajapaksa while we're on this mission," replied Rajapaksa.

"Fine. Then I want to be called Gota Shakur."

Rajapaksa sighed. Was there no one in his family besides himself who had inherited any sense?

7:55 a.m. Toronto time.

Gota and Rajapaksa got out of a cab on Markham Road in Scarborough, just north of the Macdonald-Cartier Freeway. They knew the offices to the Canadian Tamil Congress were around here. Pulling their small suitcases with wheels on them up the grassy bank, the two brothers looked for the office building on Milner Avenue. They were pointed towards a suite by some helpful but giggling office workers. Rajapaksa assumed that they had never seen a pious Buddhist before.

The brothers entered the suite but no one was there. Beside the abandoned reception desk was a line of small backpacks in bright colours. The backpacks were small and lined in military formation against the wall, suggesting a discipline and order that spooked Rajapaksa. A stuffed tiger, its whiskered face staring benignly at them, poked out of the backpack at the very end. Closest to Rajapaksa, this tiger seemed ready to pounce. For a moment, he was back there inside the pit with the wooden stakes and the writhing infernal beast, near Sigiriya, by moonlight.

118

Rajapaksa put two and two together. "It's a terrorist cell!" he cried.

The unexpected and sudden discovery scared his brother. His voice quivering, Gota tugged at the folds of Rajapaksa's robe. "Big brother, I'm scared!"

Rajapaksa used to hate it when Gota had done this as a kid. The boy would get scared of the dark and come to him for emotional succour. "Pull yourself together!" he hissed. "You're the Secretary of Defense! What would Tupac say?"

"Hai! Hai! Hai!" came sounds from the basement.

"What are those sounds, big brother?" whispered Gota.

"Terrorists performing their terrorist rituals, obviously," declared Rajapaksa. "They're probably sacrificing a kitten. Let's go see – "

"But I'm scared," reiterated Colombo's Secretary of Defense. Honestly, he was like Scooby-Doo, shaking and trembling before going into a haunted house! Would Rajapaksa have to pick him up and carry him down the stairs?

"Hai! Hai! Hai!" chanted the terrorists in unison, stripped of their individuality, brainwashed to obey and act like machines, their indoctrination audible through the simplicity and repetition of their cries.

Rajapaksa pushed open the door, trying to make it creak as little as possible. The brothers by themselves would have made the stairs buckle and groan. Together, it was all they could do to stop the pinewood stairs from splintering and collapsing. Luckily, their shifting steps were drowned out by the kathas and choreographed movements of a class of eight-year-old Tamil girls doing karate lessons before school.

Sensei Lakshman was the master of the dojo and he ran the class for girls. His mother and sister had been killed by a mortar blast during the heavy siege of their village in the early months of 2009. Sensei Lakshman had only lost his sight but his mother and younger sister had been killed. He bore an especially poignant hatred for Rajapaksa. Lakshman channelled it by teaching karate to little girls so they could defend themselves, so they would not become victims like his poor mother and sister. On particularly maddening days, when the memories were most potent, he had the girls practice their roundhouse kicks on a punching bag with a black-and-white image of Rajapaksa's face taped to it.

Now, Sensei Lakshman may have been blind but his other senses were sharp. He acutely heard the bend and heave in the stairs as they took on their added load. Rajapaksa and his brother descended cautiously down the steps but Sensei Lakshman turned towards them and sensed their wheezing and smell as if Goebbels and Göring had walked into a Jewish deli, speaking German. The venerable sensei's blood boiled and war sirens started going off between his ears. He thrust an accusatory finger at the two intruders and yelled to his charges, "Attack!"

The eight-year-old girls stopped their kathas and turned around in slow motion. Their little black terry cloth karate robes billowed and swooped around their swivelling bodies. The ends of their belts slapped against their lengthy ponytails. They recognized the three-dimensional likeness of the face they had been practicing upon. Without question or hesitation, the class of eight-year-old Tamil girls leapt forward and aimed their roundhouses at Gota and Rajapaksa. A flurry of honed, driven eight-year-old feet slapped the two brothers' faces, bellies, and thighs. It was like being stung by a hornet's nest.

"Retreat! Retreat!" cried Field Commander Rajapaksa and the two brothers scurried up the steps, the pine groaning and moaning, and stumbled out of the office as the swarm of young hornets chased them across the parking lot.

Their suitcases long abandoned behind them, the monk and rap enthusiast hurried down the grassy knoll and tried to flag a cab.

"Hai, hai, hai!" the cries of the eight-year-old karate students pursued them, promising imminent destruction and a world of pain.

"Let's split up, bro!" panted Gota. He took some sachets of bubble gum he had in his FUBU jacket pocket and threw them in the air. The gum scattered as it fell to the ground and the little hornets stopped to pick up the sweet sweet sugar. Gota had a natural instinct for eluding Tamils and Rajapaksa realized it had not diminished in the intervening years.

"Okay, you're right – they won't be able to pursue us both," he wheezed. "What are you going to do?"

"I'll take a bus," replied Gota and ran after a red-and-white TTC bus which slowed at a nearby stop. "Good luck, bro!"

Rajapaksa picked up the folds of his robe and began running again. He saw a large SUV stop at the red light across the street and ran for it. A large burly man sat in the front seat, texting furiously while others honked their horns around him. The girls came sprinting to the intersection but the light had changed against them. Having been taught to observe crossing lights and to guard themselves against 'stranger danger,' they opted not to run through traffic.

Grabbing the door of the SUV and pulling it open, Rajapaksa jumped inside. "Go, go!" he yelled, "I'll pay you anything! Just get me out of here!"

The burly man stopped texting and turned around, twisting his lips in surprise and alarm. The straw-blond spikes in his crewcut seemed to jump up in alarm from his head. "Why? What's going on? Is it the goddamned press?"

Dropping his cellphone, the man slammed the accelerator to the floor and peeled rubber. Rajapaksa barely had time to close the door before the dark SUV growled and leapt through the red light like a cat whose legs had become spinning wheels in a cartoon.

Slowly, Rajapaksa got the burly man to ease off on the pedal and explained the situation to him: he was an important politician from Sri Lanka who had escaped narrow capture by terrorists. He'd been separated from his brother and must find him again.

"Well, pleased to meet you, buddy, I'm Rob Ford," the man extended his hand and Rajapaksa shook it limply. The man looked at him with a sparkle in his eye; was Rajapaksa supposed to recognize the name?

"The mayor of Toronto? That's the city you're in, buddy!" Rob Ford slapped him on the back. "Anyway," Rob Ford raised a thick finger to his lips, "keep it under your hat! I'm skipping out on a council meeting right now."

Ford took them onto the 401 and then downtown. Rajapaksa sat there in uncomfortable silence while Ford played a mixed CD of his own design that featured the hits of The Monkees. There were an especially large number of variations of "Last Train to Clarksville" on the CD. Rajapaksa wasn't sure but he thought that the last version was sung by Ford himself who plunked along awkwardly on an out of tune guitar. It was hard to tell as Ford sang along to all the songs as they barrelled down the highway anyway, and so every song inevitably sounded like his own.

Take the last train to Clarksville
and I'll meet you at the station
We can be here by 4:30

I'll make a reservation

They stopped at a bike lane downtown near City Hall and Rob Ford eyed it ruefully. He got out and got Rajapaksa to help him measure it with a tape measure he fished from the mess of fast food wrappers and football gear strewn over the back seat. Rajapaksa held one end of the tape measure while Rob Ford measured the width of each bike lane. *Hmm,* thought Rajapaksa to himself, *we could just barely fit our tanks through here if we invade. They'd have to take up both lanes and the drivers are going to have to learn to drive on the other side.* But he kept his thoughts to himself and let Ford talk and talk and eventually, being the blabbermouth he was proving to be, Ford would reveal all his secrets and play his hand.

Rob Ford let the tape measure slide back into its roll with a satisfied snap and waved it around in the air before putting it back in his pocket. In its place, he pulled out a folded piece of paper, well-worn and greasy, with a colour film still printed on it. "You know what this is?" he asked.

Rajapaksa, who had been continuing his study of classic Hollywood films with Herath and the other ministers, instantly recognized the image of Stephen Boyd as Messala from 1959's *Ben Hur.* It was a picture of the Roman tribune riding his deadly chariot with blades attached to the chariot wheels, ready to grind and demolish the opposition.

"This is what Georgio Mammoliti and I are working on right now. They won't let us get rid of bike lanes? They haven't realized that cyclists are a pain in the *ass*? Okay, okay, well, I'm gonna let you have at it another way. We're going to pass a bill that allows motorists to attach blades to the hubs of their SUVs. And... George and I are going to do a little start-up business making blades in China and selling them to rim shops here to accessorize people's SUVs. Your pal Hu Jintao is helping us out. He's here in town to meet with us today."

"Is that correct?" asked Rajapaksa in disbelief, thinking about the personal laptop that the Chinese had given him and the space centre that was scheduled to be built near Hambantota port. Was there anything that Hu Jintao did not have his hand in?

"Hey man, you've been to Scarborough – you know how it is, right? Goddamn pinko cyclists! Roads are made for drivers, am I right?" Rob Ford picked up a discarded pop can from the floor and waited until a cyclist zoomed by and then lobbed it at her. The can bounced off a helmet guard and the cyclist briefly turned her beewaxed, dreadlocked head around and then kept cycling.

"Hu Jintao calls me 'fat boy'," said Rajapaksa dejectedly a little later. "He doesn't say it if anybody else is around but when we're alone, he calls me 'fat boy' pretending it's a term of endearment: 'how's my little fat boy doing?' Then he says something in Chinese and sits there cackling. They gave us the money for the ports and other things but I don't know... it's so humiliating."

"Don't worry about it, buddy," soothed Rob Ford and patted his new friend on the shoulder with a kind and compassionate gesture. "They make fun of my weight all the time, too. It's cruel. I got called a 'fat fuck' once. That's worse than 'fat boy', right? The worst are Joe Mihevic and Adam Vaughan. Those pinko commies come into my office and taunt me all the time. Adam Vaughan comes in and pretends that he sees Han Solo frozen in carbonite on my wall and then pulls out his wallet and offers to buy it. Do you know how humiliating that is? Hey, isn't this Queen Street? Vaughan's office must be around here somewhere."

At the news of Rob Ford's trouble with weight, Rajapaksa's coolness broke down. It may be easy for you to laugh while reading this in your snug armchair at home, but Rajapaksa was far from home and separated from the only family and friend he had been travelling with. His robe began to itch and its folds bunched up around his thighs. Now, here was a fellow victim who had suffered just as he had. Worse, the city councillors and citizens called him names to his face; apparently Ford hadn't yet mastered the art of drive-by assassinations, white van abductions, and torture camps free from the eye of the nosy press. Maybe there were a few things that Rajapaksa could teach this poor, shaky voiced pale face with the bad crewcut. Despite his original intentions, he was starting to like this hefty fellow with a penchant for speaking his mind and passion for motorists' rights. Already, he was beginning to forget the plans to invade this white man's republic, and the colony he proposed to set up in Little Eelam seemed far away.

"Man, you know what you need?" asked Rob Ford. "When I get the uglies, I just take a little," (he mimicked puffing a few tokes with his fingers) "and it lifts my spirits right up again. Sometimes I do it while I'm driving so I can face going into work." Rajapaksa had no idea what Ford was talking about but he was curious. "I especially need a little help when I have to face Adam Vaughan. I really hate that guy!"

"Let's steal something from him!" cried Rajapaksa.

The two men snuck into Adam Vaughan's office. Rajapaksa felt an echo of the same feeling he had felt earlier that morning when Gota and he had stolen into the Canadian Tamil Congress office. Though they were in a completely different part of the city right now and everything looked and smelled and sounded different, Rajapaksa had the same sense of unease in his gut, the taste of vinegar on his tongue. Runnels of sweat trickled down his thighs and made his robe damp. He could hear the buzz of the hornet's nest; the bruises from the kicks and roundhouses colouring his flesh hurt anew.

Yet he knew it was different. This was not the same pressure and frustration that he felt with his exceedingly weird and increasingly unstable younger brother. This was a man, a lummox of a man to be sure, but one who did not care about anything. He was blissfully unaware of how much people hated him. He knew it and yet did not realize it. His skin was as thick as that of a rhinoceros, not painfully sensitive like Rajapaksa's. He was happy being fat and he didn't care who knew it. Perhaps this was the true gift and asset of people in the West, their bristling confidence and disregard for the consequences of their actions. Ford, like the rest of them, floated on a sea of privilege. Rajapaksa had struggled his whole life to attain that privilege yet was not completely comfortable with it.

However, there was something foolish in this recklessness, something deliriously intoxicating. It was the craziness of his brother Gota without the baggage. Rajapaksa wanted a taste of it, even if they must pay for it; even if the taste of honey was theirs only for a moment, it was worth braving the hornet's nest. Commander Rajapaksa felt as giddy as a schoolboy, his mission now long forgotten. They were two schoolboys playing hooky, the sweetness of their freedom made even sweeter by the knowledge that it must end.

Rajapaksa distracted Adam Vaughan's secretary, pretending to be a foreign Buddhist dignitary who didn't understand much English, while Rob Ford waited outside in the hall. Rajapaksa got the poor frustrated secretary to go get someone who could help or translate and Rob Ford fixed his eyes on the large Olivetti industrial typewriter that stood idle in the corner. No one had used it for a while and its heavy khaki casing had much dust upon its shell. "Let's take that!" whispered Rob Ford, tiptoeing into the office and picking it up.

The machine was heavy and the carriage slid back with a *ching*, calling attention to them.

"Hurry, Raja!" cried Rob Ford and the two portly men, trying to cradle the beast as best they could, carried the typewriter out to the hall and over to the elevator.

They successfully got it down to the lobby and then sticking to the walls, carried the typewriter out to Queen Street and then dawdled east along to where the pawnshops were.

A pawnbroker gave them fifteen dollars for it.

"That's not much, is it?" asked Rajapaksa.

"It's freedom, baby!" cried Rob Ford. "Come on, Jarvis Collegiate is near here. I know someone there who'll sell us weed!"

On the way up Jarvis, Rob Ford and Rajapaksa obtained some makeup at a store selling Halloween face paint and painted their faces in jagged masks to look like band members from KISS. Rob Ford smeared some dark mascara around Rajapaksa's eyes in Alice Cooper streaks. "This is what the kids are wearing today," he reassured Rajapaksa. Rajapaksa now looked like a Goth monk.

They journeyed up Jarvis and Rob Ford scowled at where the bike lanes were proposed to run. Rajapaksa told Rob Ford about his wife and what a shrew she had turned out to be. When he had courted her, she had been coy, having once attained the title of Miss Sri Lanka 1973. He had gone to see her in her backstage dressing room while she was still reaping the rewards of the beauty queen circuit, and knocked on her dressing room door with a bouquet of flowers in his hand. She took the bouquet happily and placed them with the others on a shelf. He had heard that she had a history of lovers but chose not to believe it. He was sure that the other bouquets were from fans and family.

He had been very nervous in those days and hesitant. In the future, his star would rise as a lawyer. He would cement his reputation in the halls of the UN, pleading for the crimes against the JVP to be addressed. Oh, how the tables had turned! How ironic was the pen that wrote life! Shiranthi was the first woman to not make fun of his moustache and belly and he liked that about her. But he was still not sure how to win her over, how to make the moves, how to make her his own.

"If you don't like my mangoes, why then do you shake my tree?" she had coyly enquired, tracing a finger around the wattle of his chin.

"This is what I think of your mangoes!" he cried lustily and grabbed her breasts through her blouse and jiggled them up and down.

He wanted to bite into those juicy mangoes more than anything in those days and he removed the pallu of her sari, unhooked the hooks of her blouse but when he got down to the bra, he fiddled and fiddled but could not get the clasps undone. He tried rubbing them this way and that, up and down, into the plastic, stretching the fabric. Nothing worked. He was so close to those mangoes yet so far!

"Get it off!" cried Shiranthi.

He had to run into the changing room of the dressing room next door and come back with a pair of scissors and then cut the straps while she yelled at him for ruining her expensive Playtex bra.

"Why couldn't she just take it off instead of yelling at me?" groaned Rajapaksa.

"They come off?" asked Rob Ford, surprised.

Rob Ford's drug dealer was also playing hooky. He was twelve, skipping math class in the seven-eight school down the road, and learning how to apply his arithmetic in the real world. His pimply scarred face reminded Rajapaksa of the last time he had seen photos of the broken and torn earth in the North and East of Sri Lanka after the war. The drug dealer was white, had freckles and sallow skin, and wore a yarmulke. Rajapaksa didn't understand this crazy place. Why wasn't this boy being caned by the teachers for leaving school without permission?

Rob Ford bought a tiny joint off the skinny pimply boy – so tiny that Rajapaksa could barely make out what it was – and bumped fists with his drug dealer. "Until next time, my brother," wheezed Ford.

"Toda lecha Elohim," intoned the boy and routinely tucked Ford's ten-dollar bill into a gold sequined change purse which he touched to his forehead before disappearing down the street.

Rajapaksa was disturbed at how young the boy was. "What's... your dealer's... name?" he struggled to ask between their first tokes.

"Bernie... Mandelbaum..." wheezed Rob Ford. "He's saving up... for his... bar mitzvah...."

They smoked the joint underneath the bleachers and watched the football game. Their stubby fingers could hardly grasp the roach and they often dropped it and had to pick it up as quickly as they could and puff hard to keep it from going out.

At first, the roach made them morose and reflective.

"I'm a bad man," sighed Rajapaksa, "the Buddha will never welcome me so I get as much as I can while I'm on this Earth, this lifetime. I pretend to be the voice of my people but I use them to get what I want."

"No, I'm worse than you are," claimed Rob Ford. "I'm just the mayor but I treat this city as if it's my playground. The truth is, sometimes I don't even need to talk on the phone. I scroll through and look for people to call while I'm driving just because I know I can get away with it. Would I want a driver for my car? Hell, yes, but then it would take away all the fun and havoc."

"I'm despicable," sobbed Rajapaksa, "when my brother Gota was young, I'd get the others to hold him down and then fart onto his face to make sure he understood his place. I'm surprised he hasn't killed me in my sleep. Sometimes, I feel like I'd welcome it. Once, when he was staying over, I picked up his toothbrush and scrubbed my toilet with it and then put it back for him to use."

"Oh, I have a brother, too!" groaned Rob Ford, "Aren't they the worst? He's always talking about being an ethical vegetarian, so holier-than-me, so I had the wife work some chicken into the stuffing for his Tofurkey this Thanksgiving! Ha ha!"

"No, no, I really am the worst!" cried Rajapaksa, "My brother Basil is nicknamed Mr. Ten Percent because he takes ten percent of all government contracts as a commission. If they weren't too scared to nickname me, I'd be Mr. Eighty Percent. Ha! My father should be proud – I never got eighty percent a single time in my life when I was in school and now here I am! Using the country as my own personal Swiss bank, and my father's disgusted with me."

"I lied about my weight loss for charity," said Rob Ford. "I claimed to lose fifteen pounds but I actually gained weight and then used the charity money to have my own little ribs fest and ended up gaining even more weight."

"I killed maybe forty thousand innocent civilians in the last months of the war, just because I could."

Rob Ford paused for a moment, not knowing what to say to that. "Okay, you win, you're the worst," he acknowledged.

They toked for a while in silence and watched the cheerleaders on the field, their pom-poms bouncing to the flailing strands of their copper and auburn hair.

"This is really good shit," exclaimed Rob Ford, emphatically trying to compensate for how badly things were turning out.

"Where's it from?" asked Rajapaksa. He wasn't sure he was feeling anything.

"I think it's from Asia, man," said Rob Ford.

"Asia's a continent, not a country," replied Rajapaksa.

"I know, man, I know. It's beautiful!"

Rajapaksa suddenly became sad and thought of his wife Shiranthi. She was probably at home, asleep now. She would have ordered all the servants to clean things spotlessly and then to clean them again. She was a merciless woman. Still, he was on the other side of the world and

131

he suddenly missed her. Her hair like a porcupine's pelt, her large behind, and the way she bustled around smiling and nodding at everybody while seething with hatred and impatience within.

He remembered when he was young and they were newly married. She wanted children but for the first time in his life, he was making progress as a lawyer.

He didn't have time to raise kids. There was too much that was important in the country, too much to do! Once, Shiranthi was extremely sweet to him and cooked him dinner herself and washed his feet, rubbed his shoulders with linseed oil. They sent the servants away and then made love underneath the tamarind tree in the backyard. She took him in her mouth for the first time then; she had always refused to in the past. As he came in her mouth, he cried "I am King Dutugemunu!"

"Give me a second – let me go rinse this out," she mumbled and disappeared.

He learnt later that she had gone to the kitchen and spat out his sperm into a plastic container which she then refrigerated. The next day she took the container and herself to a fertility clinic and nine months later, their first son, Namal, was born. They both learned something through the process. Shiranthi had learned how hardy her husband's sperm was and Rajapaksa had learned what his wife was capable of.

Rajapaksa began to cry. After that episode, what was the point? What was the point of anything?

"Hey, hey, buddy, don't get like that," whispered Ford and shook him by the arm. "It's just the wacky tabacky man, it's not you... just look at the cheerleaders, they'll cheer you up."

Rajapaksa looked up at the teenage whores. Was nothing sacred here? Sound the death knell! Life was not for the living! Virginity was no longer virginal and innocence was no longer innocent!

Rob Ford could sense that Rajapaksa was having a really bad trip and stood him up as best as he could, brushed the grass and dirt from his robe, and walked him around. They came to a tree and Rob Ford sat Rajapaksa down in front of it. Ford pulled out a Swiss Army Knife which was attached to his keychain. He opened the toothpick and picked his teeth as if he'd momentarily forgotten what they were doing. "I've got the munchies now," he said distractedly.

"I miss my wife," said Rajapaksa dejectedly. "I can't stand her but I miss her."

"Hey, women, aren't they the worst?" chuckled Rob Ford. "Can't live with them, can't kill yourself, am I right?"

Rajapaksa burst into tears.

"Look at what I'm gonna do — this'll cheer you up!" Rob Ford opened a blade on the Swiss Army knife and then very slowly, painstakingly, carved out 'Rob + Raja' in the tree's trunk. It was an old gnarled trunk and Ford became absorbed in his work. "You and me, buddy, you and me forever!" He became so absorbed that he didn't see the school's hall monitor come out and sneak up on them.

"I've got two for the office here," said the hall monitor into his walkie-talkie, startling both Rajapaksa and Rob Ford. He pulled them both up by the scruff of their necks, in their KISS makeup, reeking of bad weed, and having carved their names into a tree. As far as the hall monitor was concerned, this would brighten up his tedious afternoon.

Ford tried to explain that they were in grade thirteen and looked old for their age but the hall monitor told him that grade thirteen had been abolished in the late nineties.

They were taken to the principal's office and then from there to 51 Division where they were locked up in holding cells.

"Don't you know who I am?" screamed Rob Ford as they were dragged down to the holding area and thrust into separate cells. "I'm the mayor! I fucking rule this city!"

"I don't know," said the first cop quietly. "I don't read the newspaper."

"Hey, Cheech," smiled the cop's partner, directing his comments towards Rajapaksa, "you want to tell Chong here to settle down?"

Rajapaksa and Rob Ford extended their pinkies through the bars separating their cells and wrapped the tips of their fingers around one another's. Trying to keep from crying, they sang the song by The Monkees that Rob Ford had taught Rajapaksa earlier:

Take the last train to Clarksville
and I'll meet you at the station
We can be here by 4:30
I'll make a reservation
don't be slow
no no no no noooo

no no no no noooo....

Shut up!" cried the other inmates.

"I'm the mayor and I'll do what I want, goddammit!" yelled Ford. "I'll play my guitar while this city burns, goddamn you!"

They finally figured out who Rajapaksa was and they got him in a car, discreetly, to meet his brother who had been found and was being held at Pearson Airport. Out of sheer malice, they pretended not to realize who Rob Ford was and decided to hold him a little longer. As they escorted Rajapaksa out in bracelets, he looked back at his counterpart, the merry pale face who was named for that great Scots rebel, Robert the Bruce. He felt sad that they were being separated, as if they were classmates who would destroy their own lives and those of others if they were allowed to share adjoining seats.

Rob Ford smiled back at him with a cheery grin that refused to quit. "Hey, don't worry about me, buddy, you had fun, right? Let me know when you're coming back. Mel Lastman and George Mammoliti and I are gonna go cruising for hookers on Toronto Island to prove that prostitution exists at Hanlan's Point. I walk up to them and ask 'Have you driven a Ford lately?' Although the last time, I ended up being beaten by an Italian housewife's purse. Still, you should come – it'll be fun!"

Rajapaksa looked at the mighty titan in wonder. The man was only halfway through his term. Rajapaksa was approaching his third term of how many? The future, with its endless days and nights, the slow wheel turning on its yoke of sovereignty, weighed heavily upon his brow...

He was actually happy to see his brother for once. Even if their mission was a failure, at least they'd gotten a free trip out of it. The roads ran on the wrong side in Scarborough, everything was spaced far apart, the food was bad, and nobody had any shame or decency over here – was the country really worth invading?

Dalton McGuinty had gotten on the phone with Stephen Harper and the two quickly arranged for a connecting flight to take the two scouts out of the country and back to their own. The last thing the two leaders wanted, especially with McGuinty on the way out, was an international incident.

Rajapaksa rubbed the KISS makeup off and thought of his fine fat fuck of a friend Rob Ford waiting in that cell for them to let him out. Would that be his own fate one day? Never! He was Rajapaksa, latest in a long line of Singhala warriors and kings, and destiny would hold a different end for him. Then he thought of the tree on the school grounds in which they had carved their names and his heart softened.

"I love you, Gota," he said to his younger brother and patted his knee. But the poor man, exhausted and worn out from the day's adventures, was asleep in his seat while the 2Pac music continued to play from his Dr. Dre headphones.

Kola Kandha (Leaf Porridge)

Well, this is the last recipe I'll be giving you. I wasn't sure if I should do it after I read the final story. It gives me no pleasure to aid and abet the contents of these stories but at least I'm at peace and beyond all this sordidness. Death is the only thing that gives peace in this life. Mahinda loves the peaceniks and laughs at their prancing and prattling about, holding hands and kissing each other fondly like sweethearts. He says, "They plant the trees and I reap the harvest. They plant trees in the ground and then also plant their own heads in the sand!"

But enough! I have a sense of humour and indulgence like everybody else but enough is enough! Do all these things really need to go into print? When I was alive, only good things, holy things, went into books. They were used to teach children and bring them up. Now, they'll print anything if it means a fast rupee. The wickeder the story, the better!

In any case... I said I would do it and I don't renege on my promises. Let it not be said that death stopped a Rajapaksa! So here I am providing the final recipe. I hope everyone understands that I'm doing it under protest. This is the most Singhalese, distinctly non-Tamil dish in the book and you're going to have to look hard to get all the appropriate ingredients. So!

Ingredients:
¼ lbs of gotukola leaves
¼ lbs of mukuanna leaves
¼ lbs of haathaavariya leaves
¼ lbs of iramasu leaves and flowers

curry leaves

1 cup of rice

2 cups of coconut milk

½ teaspoon of salt

Wash and finely cut all the greens: gotukola, mukuanna, haathaavariya, iramasu, and curry leaves. In a blender, add water to the greens and blend everything to a fine pulp. Strain the blended mixture with a fine strainer. Set this aside and boil 1 cup of rice in water for 15 mins. Once the rice has cooked, add 2 cups of coconut milk and bring the rice to a boil. Add salt and the blended greens and simmer for several minutes. Make sure you drink it hot!

Rajapaksa in Space

Flight Commander Rajapaksa stood out on the loading platform and waved to all the people gathered there, cheering, waving flags, encouraging him on. His kurakkan shawl was draped around the padded shoulders of a golden yellow spacesuit. He held his goldfish bowl helmet tucked underneath his right arm while he waved back with his left. Rajapaksa grinned and waggled his moustache with delight. He knew that Gota's goons had roused all these nearby villagers and citizens at gunpoint to come out to the new space shuttle launch pad at Hambantota port but still, it was the thought that counted. They had had to be roused and forced out of their houses in the middle of the night but this was when the launch was scheduled.

It was amazing how fast and feverishly Rajapaksa's youngest son Rohitha had worked with Gota, in concert with the Chinese of course, to set up the Ruhuna Magampura Space Centre. Right now, it only boasted a single launch pad and space shuttle but who knew what the future held? It had seemed like a dream but now, Rajapaksa was truly going to be the first Sri Lankan cosmonaut, the first Singhalese man in space. The recent satellite Supreme Sat 1 had presented a challenge but now, the frontiers of space were thrown open! The doorway to the infinite beckoned.

Simba I, Sri Lankan Space Systems' first space shuttle on Sri Lankan soil, stood erect and pointed toward the heavens. It was flanked by two beautiful external fuel tanks and two Solid Rocket Boosters, protecting it like some combustive Praetorian Guard. The whole assembly was painted a tawny colour to resemble a crouching lion, ready to spring upwards into the sky. Rajapaksa had specified that they should place accents at the tips of the shuttle to give it a snout, ears, and mane. The forward-facing windows looked like eyes and he, like a crouching homunculus, could look out at the undiscovered future. The undiscovered country and colonies awaited him. Very soon, if everything went well, SriLankan Airlines would be able to fly day trips out to Venus and Mars.

The destination of *Simba I* was the constellation Leo of course, specifically the bright star in the lion's tail, Denebola or Beta Leonis as it was sometimes called. A mere thirty-six light years away, the Chinese had installed a warp drive that Rajapaksa did not understand but operated on the understanding that it was the cutting edge of futuristic technology. Rajapaksa would be placed in suspended animation after *Simba I* had cleared the solar system's gravitational pull. Then, the Autonomous Navigational System built by the Chinese would kick in and move the ship into warp speeds. They would move through wormholes at speeds approaching the speed of light so that Rajapaksa would not be a much older man by the time he reached his destination. The whole framework of the shuttle, and Rajapaksa, would be converted to energy so that it could move forward and then be reconstituted into a matter matrix once the shuttle's quantum approached Denebola. *Denebola.* Rajapaksa rolled the word around his mouth with delight. It sounded vaguely Singhalese. He just hoped that the Chinese had got everything right. He'd hate for something to go wrong while they took apart his molecules and atomic forces and reassembled them into the glory that would be Emperor Rajapaksa the First. He'd hate for them to build these space shuttles like they did his cellphone – he had dropped it into the toilet the other day and once he fished it out, the LCD stopped functioning.

It would be strange to be gone from his family for so long (a little over four months) with no one but himself to keep counsel and maintain functions in the shuttle. Rajapaksa had been surrounded by ministers and advisors awaiting his orders, petitioners awaiting his audience, and developers awaiting his favour. He had not been alone a single moment of a single day for years now. Even at night, his wife demanded this or that of him, while he tried to get a few restless hours sleep.

This was why, when the opportunity availed itself, Rajapaksa had volunteered to undertake the first mission. Everyone had praised his bravery and courage but Rajapaksa had known it would be a chance to escape the foreign dignitaries, the endless criticism of the UN and the foreign press, the sycophantic panderings of his cabinet, but most of all, his unappeased wife. Some peace and quiet for a change.

Hu Jintao had simply sent a text saying: "This space shuttle costs a lot of yen. Don't screw things up, fat boy." Gota had exercised his role on this project with uncharacteristic diligence and care. The two brothers celebrated over dinner at Gota's house the night before. There was not a single thing that Rajapaksa could find fault with in terms of plans or arrangements. Once in a while, Gota still retained the capability to surprise him.

Gota's wife threw freshly cut strips of tenderloin beef to their pet sharks while the two brothers toasted Rajapaksa's feat of daring. Rajapaksa had felt a hitherto misplaced fondness for his brother ever since they had returned from the unfruitful trip to Toronto. He had to thank his lucky stars that he was not languishing in some Toronto jail right now with urine stains on the walls and floor. Of course, he had heard about Rob Ford's troubles after the short stint in the holding cells and was not surprised. Such a reckless despot must reap reckless rewards. That's where he, Rajapaksa, had been extremely cautious. He did not smoke or drink (most of the time) and was careful whom he surrounded himself with. He was tied to everyone either by blood, fear, or favour. The blood flowed both ways while the fear and favour flowed out from him.

Best of all, he had been reunited with his brother physically and spiritually at the end of their trip to Toronto. Gota did not know it but Rajapaksa felt something for his younger difficult brother that he had not felt since Gota was merely a baby... a kind of pride and affection and softness that warmed him. It was as if the trip had finally, after all these years, brought them down to the same level, had eroded the disjunction between the two brothers that the hierarchy of political office brought. They were part of each other's lives. They were part of each other's souls.

Unfortunately, Gota was still obsessed with rap music from the nineties and 2Pac continually blared from his stereo system the whole time Rajapaksa was there, but at least Gota turned down the volume to a soft patter upon Shiranthi's insistence. Although, Gota had not been able to refrain from politely correcting his sister-in-law's pronunciation from *two-pack* to *too-pawk*. Shiranthi fumed while *too-pawk* issued from the speakers:

> *Lord help me, save me, mama keep prayin'*
> *For a young motherfucker tryin' to duck an early grave*
> *In a city where ya can't tell the snakes from the fakes*
> *Fakes from the phonies, enemies of the homies...*

Shiranthi, on the other hand, had not taken the news of Rajapaksa's flight too well. He told her that he needed a little break from the usual routine.

"You – want a *break* from me?!" she screamed, "I'll *break* your goddamn neck! Come here and I'll show you!"

Getting her used to the idea and refraining from erupting whenever the topic came up had become a titanic effort, but she had been able to maintain her icy smile for the cameras. That was most important.

Now, as the countdown ended, the boosters pushed their mixture of jet fuel and fire out their thrusters and *Simba I* slowly climbed aloft on a cloud of solid propellants, ionized air, and enterprise. A cloud of fiery flames and exhaust pushed against the launch site at Hambantota and for a moment the crowd froze, all the ships in the harbour stilled, even the birds seemed to hover in the air as all extended their eyes upward to see their glorious leader ascend to the heavens.

The glorious leader felt the ratcheting g-forces as the boosters increased their thrust, pushing Rajapaksa into the stratosphere, then into regions where the air was so thin that the fluid in his eyeballs would freeze and crack their orbs if he hadn't been protected. Rajapaksa craned to look at the images of the disappearing island at night. On the monitors, the dense hot jungles, the striking Buddhist statues, Sigiriya fort and Adam's Peak, the hustle and activity of rebuilding in the North – it all pulled away from him as if it were a receding black marble dotted with light. It was hard to see as *Simba I*'s bolts and plates rattled with the sheer forces of takeoff and for a moment Rajapaksa wondered what would happen if the shuttle did not make it. What would happen if its windows, *Simba*'s eyes, cracked like the LCD screen on his cellphone? His life was as cheap then as a poorly manufactured phone. Then he remembered that even if he did not have full confidence in Gota, his own son had worked on the project and ensured its integrity.

The boosters fell away and Rajapaksa felt a weight fall from him. It left him giddy and floating. The large tank of fuel was still carrying him upwards but his trajectory began to change, the curve became less sharp, and Rajapaksa was not thrown backwards into his seat with such force. Slowly, he unbuckled himself and took off the large golden helmet which covered his head like a fishbowl. He checked the life support systems and the auxiliary controls, made sure the wire navigational systems were working, and reported back to the command centre at Hambantota. Cameras on the outside of the shuttle gave him a distorted view of the last fuel tank decoupling and pulling away, leaving Rajapaksa and his dreams all alone in space. Despite the fiery thrust of the rockets, there was a cold blue hum that pervaded not just the vacuum but the very sound and temperature of space. It was the lack of these common elements that made him cross the ribbed arms of his tawny golden spacesuit and find his way to the rear of the shuttle. A condensed meal of space food awaited him. He had insisted that the designers create the specifications of the spacesuit to resemble those upon Hugo Drax's orbiting space station in *Moonraker* but his outfit looked more like it belonged in *Tintin: Explorers on the Moon*.

Like most Sri Lankans of a certain generation, Rajapaksa had learned about sexuality from James Bond films and *Moonraker* held a special place in his heart. The realistic special effects, the glamour of lasers, Hugo Drax's inspired plan of creating a new master race in space, spelled wonderment and magic to the younger Rajapaksa's heart. Perhaps tonight was the final fruition of that dream.

Rajapaksa had asked for all the Bond movies to be loaded into the shuttle's databases as his in-flight entertainment. Now, to distract his nerves, he clicked through the menus underneath the 'My Computer' folder and found *Moonraker*. The irony of observing the film's space sequences as he himself was flying through space was not lost upon the president. Too cruel though was the irony that Rajapaksa moved towards the end of his life while the real young Sri Lankans, the nubile, lusty, endeavouring Sri Lankans, roamed on the ground below. He was up here in the eerie desolation of space, of cold absence.

In the Bond film, Drax's colony of beautiful people, with auburn and brunette and blonde hair, coupled off in pairs of horny space cadets. Man and woman, they entered their space shuttles in pairs. The women were all so sexy and beautiful in their white mini space-skirts, all bare-legged and large-haired, the plunging necklines of their space wear revealing smooth and delectable skin. And there was Drax, what little neck he possessed lost in the collar of his Nehru shirt, permanently unimpressed, lording over them all.

Still, even the younger Rajapaksa would have preferred to have turned out to be Bond than Hugo Drax. Despite his vast wealth, formidable forces, and years of preparation and intelligence, the villain was always undone. Why was that? Rajapaksa had wished to be the Singhalese Sean Connery. The Sri Lankan sex machine. Instead he was Hugo Drax, he was Auric Goldfinger, he was Ernst Stavro Blofeld. They had almost finished the first of the Singhalese remakes of American classic movies and they styled a Singhalese Government logo for the films that resembled the MGM lion. Except, instead of having a lion roaring in the centre, they had taken footage of Rajapaksa opening his mouth wide and roaring in imitation of a lion. Rajapaksa had seen the finished logo and felt ridiculous, there in his kurakkan shawl and silk kurta, roaring like a child who wished for a lollipop. He had been too tired to tell them to scrap the logo and simply nodded his head with heavy resignation and sighed. They should have gotten Gota to be the lion, to be the Bond villain with his sharks swimming around the living room and 2Pac playing in the background. Now there was a man whom you could expect to one day acquire his own island fortress and turn out to be a Bond villain. Not Rajapaksa. Not this way. Rajapaksa was tired of it all and paused the *Moonraker* film.

He got up, disconsolate, and made his way to the kitchenette. Slowly and with care through his bulky space gloves, Rajapaksa opened the frozen kola kandha that had been simulated to resemble his mother's leaf porridge. He sipped the green paste through a straw slowly and looked out the bracketed windows, into the depths of the heavens. This was a God's eye view; this was the sight that angels saw.

Leo beckoned in the darkness and Denebola, the tail, blinked like a star from the afterlife, from the future, from the retina of Buddha himself. Rajapaksa finished the food like a good boy even though it had the consistency of putrefied shoelaces, and prepared himself for cryogenic hibernation. Soon he would enter a stasis and his matter would be converted to energy. He took one last look out the window; the shuttle was already beyond Jupiter and Saturn. The Earth was an imagined speck floating in front of the glow of the sun. And Sri Lanka? An atom on that mote of dust.

He wondered what his wife, Shiranthi, was doing right then.

*

Rajapaksa was jolted out of hibernation and woke up with a start. Why was it that with sleep, even cryogenic sleep, he woke drenched in cold sweats? Pulling the sensors off his body and forehead, Rajapaksa got up in his shorts and raised the lid of his cryogenic chamber. He was solid, as solid as he had always been. In his dream, Rajapaksa believed that he was disintegrating, his molecules scattered across the universe, mixing with those of decomposing Tamils from the killing fields. The ship shook a little and rumbled forward and Rajapaksa had to gather his thoughts.

Was he already there? Impossible! Something felt wrong. Still in his skivvies, Rajapaksa walked around and attempted to get a sense of things, rubbing the immense headache and fogginess out from his head. His throat was sandy and dry. He gazed out the windows, then recalibrated his position upon the monitors. It was true; he was light years and light years away from Earth but nowhere near Denebola. None of the constellations made any sense. The dark sky looked hostile and menacing, vast with inscrutability, cold with depth and formlessness. A few stars did glisten but these seemed so sharp and remote as to taunt him with their xenophobia. He had never taken an interest in the stars before but he marvelled at how easily he could tell that things were different, how removed he was in space and time, from everything that he knew. It unnerved him that the sky was no longer familiar or recognizable.

A large sun blazed below him, much bigger than the one at home, but it was not Beta Leonis. The shuttle still moved forward. Due to the relative size of the sun, it hardly seemed to be moving at all. Rajapaksa felt like a snail crawling across the surface of the sun. He poured himself some water, fixed himself a late night space-snack of blue paste mixed with some yellow liquid so that it started to make a sort of green gruel, combined this with some of the kola kandha and sat himself back down in front of *Moonraker*, and began to watch where he left off.

He ate the kola kandha, wiping the excess paste around his lips, and watched as Roger Moore was led into the faux stronghold of Hugo Drax, behind the waterfall. A blonde woman in a flowing dress and low neckline led him into a granite oasis that boasted Mayan accents and Eden-like decor. Slowly, as Roger Moore availed himself of the stronghold, woman after woman stepped out from hidden paradises and took their places in tableaux conference around the pool. Unknown to Roger Moore, a deadly python made its nest within the pool. The women wore their hair in permed bouffants, possessed rouged cheeks, and were painted with lurid pastel lipsticks, magnifying their lips in just the way Rajapaksa liked. Why did people no longer dress the way they had back in the late seventies, the early eighties?

As the women stared at Bond invitingly and Roger Moore returned their smiles with his sly hint of lasciviousness, and cocked a trademark eyebrow, Rajapaksa imagined himself there instead of Bond. It was not Moore but Rajapaksa who was surrounded by all those beautiful women. He imagined himself going to bed amongst their combined gorgeousness, peeling off their space garments, biting into their pale necks and succulent white breasts. He imagined himself between all of their legs, simultaneously, and then experienced something he had not felt for a long time – an erection!

And what an erection! Wearing only his skivvies like Sigourney Weaver at the end of *Alien*, his proboscis had ample room and opportunity to engorge itself. His old fervour, the primal flame he had possessed as a young man, came back to him with doubled recompense. His tumescent shaft and ripe reddish-purplish head announced themselves with a thirteen-year-old's impetuosity. Let Shiranthi say he was digging between couch cushions for change now! The Singhalese Sean Connery was back! The Sri Lankan sex machine was here!

Rajapaksa grabbed his rod and began stroking. The space food fell to the floor. He grasped the convenience of his unclothed state and clutching his chest hairs with one hand, stroked the shaft of his penis with the other and tickled his balls with his little finger. He kept one eye open, watching the action and beauty onscreen, while the other eye was closed, its orb turned toward the earthly delights of his guilty heart. The spunk welled up in him with such a life force that he had not experienced since... since... it was not until....

Suddenly, the digital image of Roger Moore wrestling with the python disappeared. There was a large click and the image was replaced with a live feed from the command base back in Hambantota. What inconvenient timing! Gota stood there, in his glasses and little moustache, fully clothed, grinning at the monitor in front of him. Hu Jintao stood beside Gota. What was Hu Jintao doing there? Hu Jintao never came to Sri Lanka – Rajapaksa always went to him. And beside them both stood Shiranthi, an embarrassed and sheepish smile curled around her lips. They had literally caught Rajapaksa with his dick in his hands.

"Hello, fat boy, enjoying yourself?" sneered Hu Jintao.

"Hello Aiya," chuckled Gota, even more menacingly than Hu Jintao.

Shiranthi said nothing.

"You're not going to Leo," announced Gotabaya. "In fact, you're not going anywhere, my dear brother. Except hell. Time to pray for your sins!"

"Sorry, fat boy," cackled Hu Jintao, "you understand, this is just business?"

"Look at him – how stupid he looks!" mocked Gota. "Well, who's the sucka now, nigga? You don't fart on my face! I fart on your face, nigga!" Gota lifted an imaginary pistol and fired a couple of rounds at the screen, imitating holding it sideways the way he had seen gangstas in films hold theirs.

"And you, too, Shiranthi?" asked Rajapaksa, wrestling with his own python that squirmed and throbbed in his embarrassed hand.

"You shouldn't have left, Mahinda... I'm sorry," whispered his wife, not able to look him in the eye.

Rajapaksa could not bear the shock and excitement any more. He exploded with surprised orgasm all over the screen. Gesticulating, he ejaculated. The glorious leader's seed burst forth and shot straight, right onto the screen. Ropes of golden sperm shot out his cannon at high velocity and struck the faces of Shiranthi, Gota, and Hu Jintao smack dead in the centre. The spunk, thick and viscous, first held to the magnified faces on the screen then began to slide, and then dripped down the monitor, heavy with wet weight.

"What did he do?" asked Hu Jintao, livid with rage.

"I think he just came on our faces," replied Shiranthi wistfully. "I had forgotten what that feels like...."

"No matter," snarled Gota, "we'll get the last laugh yet, older brother. That billion-dollar space craft you're riding? It'll be the last thing you ever see. It's a billion dollar coffin, understand? It's going to explode in space right now and it's going to take you in pieces with it. I'm pressing the remote self-destruct button right now! Adieu, my brother. Adieu, motherfucka!"

The image on the screen blinked out, bringing Roger Moore and the python back onto the screen, leaving Rajapaksa in a state of total powerlessness and panic. What should he do? What could he do? Suddenly the shuttle came to a jarring stop, decelerating and slamming Rajapaksa against the wall. A computerized warning siren blared: "Auto self-destruct sequence initiated. This spacecraft will self destruct in T-minus ten seconds. T-minus nine seconds...."

An escape pod! Rajapaksa had to find an escape pod so he could eject from the space shuttle in time but alas... it was a space shuttle! There *was* no eject pod! What was he going to do?

"T-minus eight seconds, t-minus seven seconds...."

Was this the end? Did all the back room intimidating, the secret slaughtering, the denials of wrongdoing and the setting up of secret bank accounts, lead to this? He had worked for a generation to make himself dominant, impregnable. He was just learning to love his brother and wife again. Why did it have to come to this?

"T-minus six seconds, t-minus five seconds...."

Why did he not connect the dots and see this coming? Gota throwing himself into all aspects of the Leo mission. Gota becoming disturbed when they read the excerpt from the *Raging Bull* script.

"T-minus four seconds, t-minus three seconds...."

Gota pretending to be overly afraid during their trip to Scarborough, engineering things so he could be conveniently separated from his brother in a foreign country that

Hu Jintao visited. The graffiti on the mirror wall at Sigiriya rock!

"T-minus two seconds...."

Unknown to Rajapaksa, his glorious ropes of sperm which had splashed the large monitor and slid down the console had healthily, silkily, stealthily, worked their way in between the control panels and into the wiring of the ship. If his erection had been any less urgent, or the eruption less vital, he might have died there and then. The Rajapaksa legacy would have come to a swift end.

But he was not fated to perish in the cold tombs of space, alone, unloved, and unmourned. The sperm bore the ebullience of his genetic code, the strange mixture of machismo and magic that is Rajapaksa, and while some of it still lay congealed upon the screen, other globules were hardy enough to penetrate to the very core of the ship's controls. With an obdurate resistance to fate, these squiggles of spunk surrounded the auto-destruct mechanism and gummed up the works.

The computer voice announcing the countdown slowed down to a roll: "T-minus one..." and then stopped completely.

Rajapaksa was saved!

But then, his spunk, after gumming up the works, stopped the wire systems from working altogether and the shuttle began to nosedive. It fell into freefall, spinning through space. The simulated gravity fell away and Rajapaksa was suddenly weightless in his sticky skivvies while the shuttle fell towards the immense gravity of the Class I star below him. If he did not act quickly, he would know intimately what it meant to be part of the nuclear fusion process.

The deserted imitation kola kandha began to rise and float in the air above him. He pushed it aside and made for where his tawny spacesuit hung on a hook. The semen that still lay dripping on the screen in front of him congealed into discrete sticky balls of different sizes and floated off the screen, now freed from gravity. The sperm globules, each spherically perfect, seemed to swim through weightless air and propel themselves toward him like children seeking their parent. Rajapaksa brushed some of them aside with his arms but they clung to the hair on his chest, and lodged themselves into his moustaches, his hair plugs, his nape. There was no time to think about the grossness now or take the time to wash it off. Rajapaksa floated/swam towards the golden suit shimmering in front of him and stripping off his sticky skivvies, forced himself into the tailored glittering armour. He picked the fishbowl helmet up and placed it over his head, snapped shut the airtight clasps. Wrapped the kurakkan shawl around his neck. The oxygen pump kicked in and he slowly acclimatized to breathing in such a contained space.

Even in his suit, he could feel the heat build up within the cabin of the space shuttle. The faces of the dials glowed red instead of black and the air was starting to roast him as if he were in a kiln. With no time to waste, Rajapaksa fiddled with the controls of the emergency explosive bolts on the door hatches. He must ignite them before the controls melted! He could feel his hair getting singed and falling to crisps on his body. The skin itself was becoming dry, leathery, and scarred. Only the molecular integrity of the suit stopped its mesh from falling apart and disintegrating. His skin felt as if he were on fire. With a sustained act of will, Rajapaksa ignited the primary charges on the door bolts and the door immediately shot out into space, the cold vacuum sucking out some of the heat and friction from the spacecraft.

It would almost be too late if Rajapaksa did not act very, very quickly. He grabbed the nearest fire extinguisher and jumped out of the gaping airlock. He immediately activated the extinguisher, propelling himself upwards, against the momentum of the space shuttle. *Simba I* continued to fall towards the unknown sun until it became trapped in its massive orbit and then simply vanished, disappearing among the flames of the sun's photosphere and chromosphere.

Rajapaksa heaved a sigh of relief, exhausting the contents of the extinguisher until nothing hissed out anymore. He abandoned the canister which bobbed amiably in space and then took his first look around. At some point, the kurakkan shawl had unwrapped itself from his suit and he watched it flutter off into the void. *There it goes*, he whispered to himself.

The view was magnificent. To fly, to be aloft, even to be the tiniest speck in the heavens, was truly incredible. The Magellenic clouds of stardust drifted away from him in the Milky Way to grant a view he had not been able to see from the space shuttle. Solar flares leapt up from the surface of the sun. Planets, green streaked with cerulean attendants, circled the sun like a nest of cubs feeding at their mother. All his power and might was stripped away from him but what a sight had been granted! A sight that not two in six and a half billion had seen! He had had to lose all his influence and accumulated wealth to see this wondrous sight and he would pay that price again, pay the price a thousand times over, to live, to fly, to see the glories of this wonderful universe its creator had bestowed.

He knew he could not live long. Already, all the hair on his body was singed and gone. His flesh was scarred and charred. In any case, it had changed colour. He was sure that not even his mother would recognize him now. Soon, the air supply would run out and then the immensity of death that was held without would come flooding in, the water in his body would evaporate, and his eyeballs would crack. The ligaments in his joints would collapse and his bones would shrivel up as if he were a mummy, just like Gota had promised. He floated there above the magnificent veld of the universe but what was he to do?

Once again, fate was on Rajapaksa's side. He could not know this but though he could see nothing around him in the vast reaches of space above the Class I star, the ether was actually densely populated by waveforms of an alien species that, were we to try to transliterate their native names right here in English, would take at least three and a half pages. And our publisher is quite annoyed at the length of this particular story as it is. So, suffice it to say that there were the eggs of invisible alien life forms swimming around him, somewhat like translucent jellyfish at the bottom of the darkest oceans, unobserved but there in a very real sense. Now, these alien waveforms weren't predatory or parasitic exactly but something else we do not have a word for in our language. They propagate through space in their sector looking for gametes from other life forms to couple with. The waveforms themselves do not possess any gender but harvest the ideas and sensibilities of the gametes they couple with, like some literary publicists that I know. The aliens do the coupling quite quickly and the process is invisible and insensible in its own right. What are we talking about? Well, some of the Rajapaksa sperm which clung to his hair and moustaches had floated free into the contained atmosphere of the shuttle and then into the void, still alive, propelling their little golden flagella through space, when Rajapaksa had blown the explosive bolts.

Rajapaksa had already learned how hardy his sperm could be through the circumstances that led to the conception of his first son. Though its use had become attenuated over the years, the Rajapaksa spermatozoa itself had not lost its hardiness or constitution. In fact, if anything, like a prisoner whose anger and vitality is continually kindled by being held without trial in a government camp, this rare breed of sperm was that much more intensified by the neglect in Rajapaksa's dotage. These dynamic and hardy Rajapaksa seed, when finally released, were to couple with the waveforms and transform into some very interesting and dynamic beings of their own, although Rajapaksa himself had no idea what was going on. He would view the ripened seeds of these strange progenitations as a series of intense visions. We now return you to him.

Rajapaksa woke up in the deep vacuum of space. The air was beginning to go and he felt his charred body cooling. The rivers and streams of his body where the blood carried life were beginning to wither and dry up. He thought that since he was to die anyway, he might as well take off his golden goldfish bowl of a helmet and experience the grandeur of space directly with his own orbs. The naked eyes. Let he and the infinite become one. The helmet came off with some difficulty and Rajapaksa allowed it to drift away, like so many things. He felt the top of his head and was relieved rather than surprised to find he had gone completely bald. He was as smooth as a baby. The moustache that he had carried like a burden, constantly weighing his upper lip down in a frown, had disintegrated and it was delicious to feel the coolness of space over that denuded upper lip, that hairless translucent dome.

Why was he not dead? Why was he not dying? Rajapaksa felt something alive around him but could not say what it was. Was it the portal to the afterworld that he had sometimes dreamt of? Nirvana. Was he, hope against hope, wretch beyond wretches, to see the Lord Buddha after all?

A strange apparition floated before him, giant and mighty and looming in space. It obscured the sun and had not been there a moment before. Where did it come from? Three giant aunties, dark Tamil ladies now in the autumn of their lives, stirred the contents of a metal vessel over a clay oven. They wore bright orange and green saris that stood luminous against the starred welkin of the sky. A fourth, the queen of the bunch, directed their ministrations with an old hand much weighed down with bangles. He recognized the women from the dread dream he had while staying at the hotel in London – these were the dark aunties that met weekly to criticize and cajole, to congratulate and condemn.

"Fair is foul and foul is fair..."

"...in Sri Lanka's fog and filthy air!" chanted the weird aunties as they threw dahl, chilies, garlic, turmeric, and cardamom into their pot.

"How now you black and midnight darkies!" cried Rajapaksa, "What is it you do, and why have you brought me here?"

The women cackled and turned their attention towards him: "We cook a dish without a name!"

"Hail to thee, Rajapaksa, Leader of the Opposition!" cried the first dark aunty.

"Hail to thee, Rajapaksa, Prime Minister of Sri Lanka," cried the second weird aunty.

"Hail to thee, Rajapaksa, less than President but greater than all others!" laughed the third, producing tittering notes that seemed to scorn Rajapaksa's current condition.

Their forms flickered and wavered in space.

"Stay, you imperfect creatures!" shouted Rajapaksa through his fear. "If you can look into the seeds of time and say what will grow and what will not, tell me of my fate! What will happen to me?"

"They cannot be commanded," stated the leader of the aunties imperiously, "but we will communicate with you, and speak of deeds without names. Would you hear it from our lips or from those of our masters?"

"Speak then!" cried Rajapaksa, "Show me!"

The aunties went back to the stirring of their pot and spoke Tamil imprecations, gargling and cackling, over their pot. A peal of thunder broke out through the heavens, lightning came down from the black sky and electrified the deep space behind the hags who soon dissipated. They ignited the mixture within the pot before disappearing. The trails of their laughter could still be heard even though they were to be seen no more.

The pot remained a little longer and seemed to sizzle and boil as steam and vapours rose from it before forms began to rise, sensual yet vague, pleasing to the eye and terrifying at the same time. They were at first faint as weak watercolours but quickly formed in mass and intensity to great brush strokes of oil and acrylic. The forms towered large above Rajapaksa. *Am I in the highest of the four heavens?* he wondered. *Is this the realm where the devas are forty-five hundred feet tall and live for almost ten billion years?*

The first being was made of alabaster marble, white and stony, as if carved out of a single piece of ivory stretching up into the heavens. Thickly hewed, its limbs moved slowly and it was bearded and wore a crown of thorns from which blood stained its lean and terrifying face. Rajapaksa had to lie back and crane his neck upwards to even get a glimpse of this gaunt, haunted face. The perspective was almost impossible. And yet, he could tell that the slow, stony, creaking being had no eyes. If it possessed eyes, it would be too terrible. Too terrible to bear!

The second being to come out of the pot was no less large but was dark in comparison, blending against the black and starry sky. Its limbs were made stringy by yogic exercise, purplish in hue with blue-black definition of the muscles. This deva wore a deerskin around his waist, had thick hair piled high, and the Ganges shot out of a crescent moon lodged high in his coiffure. His lips were dark and his eyes severe. He carried a trident with a small drum fastened to its neck.

The two beings began to circle and thunder around Rajapaksa. Every time they moved or stamped their feet, the heavens shook and the planets juddered and whirred. As the planets and celestial bodies fell back to their orbits, Rajapaksa found himself miraculously intact, still in the middle of the fracas and fray. The two beings sized each other up like WWE wrestlers and prepared to square off against each other. They locked arms and struggled to maintain the stronger hold. Finally, the dark deva lifted the alabaster sightless one and brought him crashing to the ground. The solar systems were scrambled and Rajapaksa found himself shielding his face from a barrage of meteorite fragments that spun out of control.

"Hey, watch it!" he cried.

The alabaster loser picked himself up, shook off the bits of bone and ivory that flaked off his shoulders and stepped back into the pot. Rajapaksa almost imagined him tag-teaming his partner who then rose like a congealed apparition, a baby floating in the steam, growing larger until it also was forty-five hundred feet tall and could challenge the victor.

This new being was large and mighty but also slim-limbed and with slack stomach. Wearing a saffron robe that fell in loose folds, it exuded beauty and calm and purpose. Its hair was also tied up onto its head and this was even darker than that of the alabaster deva's, making the contrast and definition palpable. The second god's ears were large and drooped to his shoulders which he flexed and stretched with ease. In his smile and eyes were a benign cunning that made Rajapaksa shiver.

The vastness of space was their mat and as there were no ropes, the ring spread out to infinity. Planets circled in their orbits, entering the space between the two beings, then passing through their bodies in a ghostly glide. A trio of comets passed up through the 'floor' and ascended in unison like a school of rocky fish.

Shiva dropped his trident, stamped his thick legs onto the 'mat' and strode forward. Solar flares erupted from nearby suns in response. Space and time coiled around these rumbling deities.

The impending clash of titans created great anguish within Rajapaksa. He did not know if he could survive it. Furthermore, he could not say why but he felt responsible... as if the entire violent and destructive spectacle were being performed specifically for his benefit. He felt each shudder, each tear of the flesh, each wrenched bone within his own body. He was like The Fisher King and the violence found its root within him.

"Stop this... stop this at once," commanded Rajapaksa with only a shadow of the authority he had once possessed. His voice was a whisper in the heavens, a prayer on the non-existent winds.

"Look who talks!" boomed the purplish-black deva.

The two beings retreated from each other slowly and crouched down to view Rajapaksa. Still, they were massive, towering over his tiny frame. Another word, another gust or a whisper from either of them, would have hurled Rajapaksa clear to the other end of the solar system.

"Shrink down to my size!" pleaded Rajapaksa, the familiar sweat streaming in runnels down his hairless body.

"Who commands?" asked the saffron-robed deva.

Rajapaksa summoned all of the will left him in his broken puny frame. "I killed a tiger once with my bare hands. I am Rajapaksa. Hear me roar!" he cried out.

The devas stepped back cautiously, broke apart, and began to dissemble. Like thick garish oil paintings changing back to the faintest of watercolour sketches, their bodies began to shimmer, their muscles unlocked. The thick sturdy limbs were soon watery and unformed. Before they dispersed, each being opened his mighty mouth and coughed up a seed. Rajapaksa thought they were going to come at him at once, charge him and rip the poor cosmonaut to pieces like a sprig or a wishbone. Instead, eggs had come out of their mouths.

These seed-like eggs were round and smooth and impossibly translucent. They bore the consistency of his new skin. As soon as they had been loosed upon the world, these eggs mocked Rajapaksa by growing follicles of hair and acquiring colour. Charged pelts of fur sprouted from the new beings' bodies. They circled each other like their predecessors. Their eyes were cat-like and moved in flickers on either side of their large noses which were wet as they licked themselves with their tongues. One developed a strong mane while the other grew striations, stripes, on his skin. How could Rajapaksa not recognize these beasts for what they were?

They now circled each other, these magnificent jungle cats, one a lion, the other a tiger. They pawed space with their claws, ready to rip constellations to shreds. They licked the blood from their wounds and roared, snuffing out suns in one go. The momentum and energy of a magnetic storm blew charged ions all around them.

"Stop!" cried Rajapaksa, "Stop this at once!"

"It is because of you," said the tiger, turning his head slowly and showing eyeballs that were as clear and milky and deathlike as pearls.

"It is all because of you," echoed the lion, who was also blind, "do you not enjoy the fruits of your victory?"

"No, no," yelled Rajapaksa. "What do you want with me?" His colon unclenched and his bowels let loose their charge within the awkward confines of his spacesuit. His bladder then followed. A warmth spread up his hairless legs.

Even in the vacuum of space, the nervous rank of Rajapaksa's waste could not be missed. As if drawn to fear, the two animals turned and strode towards Rajapaksa in tandem. He flailed within his suit, but could not evade its immobility or stink.

"If not you, who, then?" growled the lion, "Whom must we devour? Tell us who is to blame!"

"If you don't tell us the truth, we will devour you," smiled the tiger with a mouth full of teeth. A homicidal

Cheshire cat, the tiger's face loomed as large as a mountain range in front of Rajapaksa, each of the teeth a jagged peak or ridge.

"You are *my* vision," ruled Rajapaksa in a final feeble attempt to maintain authority, "I am clothed in great power and I command you to obey me."

"It would seem to me that you are clothed in shit!" hissed the tiger. The lion roared out in laughter and the two beasts shared a mirth that seemed to go on for eons.

"Ask my electorate, ask my people," whispered Rajapaksa hoarsely. "Ask them who have had peace for the first time in decades whether I did the right thing? Judge me not by my actions but by my effects!"

"Ask them yourself," chuckled the lion. The two beasts stood up straight like immense Trojan horses stretching up to the zenith and slowly, other beings began to climb out of them. Human forms, whisperish and wraith-like climbed out of the huge cats' fur, came out from between their toes, moved forward over their heads and from behind their ears as if the beasts were stony precipices that the humans were to climb down.

These forms were roughly the same size as Rajapaksa and as they hovered into view, in the centre of the ring, they did not seem to walk but floated and shimmered in midnight space. Slowly, they came into focus and Rajapaksa saw them as dark-skinned Tamils (darkies!) and the barely clothed Singhalese (his electorate!), moaning and wailing. These hordes were the inverse of those protesting and shouting mobs he had narrowly avoided in England. The mobs had shouted at him but these souls were worse: unintelligible, accusing. Instead of placards, they hoisted severed limbs and body parts. The shades were bent, doubled over, pitiful and in mourning for they bore great wounds: gouges in their eyes, heads, arms, and chests. Blood welled up in their eye sockets and mouths. Mothers carried dead babies. Old men cradled bloodless legs and arms. The halt and the lame crawled on their knees. Husbands carried deceased wives and mothers suckled dead babies which had been ripped from their bellies. Poor workers with their heads bloody, brains trickling out in a greyish-yellow goo. Muslims holding bags of flour, the last of their provisions saved from the looting and burning. A Christian woman, identifiable because of the gold crucifix hung around her neck, while the breasts below had been hacked off as war trophies. And countless others without ears, fingers, teeth, genitals, or even ribs.

"You cannot say I did it!" cried Rajapaksa, "Never shake your gory locks at me!"

"You are a sinner to the highest degree," continued the lion. "If you atoned by performing a good deed, a great deed, every hour for the rest of your life, you would not even begin to make up for all the horror and death you have caused."

"Not even the Buddha would forgive you," whispered the tiger.

"But it wasn't my fault," cried Rajapaksa. "I only ended the war."

And then one form, distinguishable from all the rest, more loving and radiant and angelic than the others, more regal in his Mickey Mouse hat and Space Mountain t-shirt, distanced itself from the crowd and came forward. It had white hair, was quite shrunken, and possessed a dried and hollow face with a sad beseeching smile playing on his lips. This being floated forward and with a pang, Rajapaksa recognized his own brother.

"Dudley!"

He was embarrassed for Dudley to see him thus, evacuated and stinking in the hot putrid warmth of his own filth. More than anything, his eyes which seemed to understand and know everything reduced the last of Rajapaksa's defenses. The last vibrating nerve, the last string in his leg, went slack and everything fell apart. His heart collapsed. "My brother, what are you doing here?"

"I am dead, of course," replied Dudley in his impossibly sad and beautiful way. "It's you that should not be here — what are you doing here?"

"How, dead?" asked Rajapaksa. "Did you... kill yourself?"

"No, no... I had some struggles... but have you not seen me? I died of old age and a broken heart over what's happened to Sri Lanka."

"Old age?" Rajapaksa looked at the shade of his brother closely, the white wisps of hair underneath the Disney World t-shirt. His slow words had the ring of truth about them, but how could this be?

"Is this my legacy, Dudley?" asked Rajapaksa, dejectedly. "Is this really what I've caused?"

"You must be honest, Aiya, with others and with yourself. No life, no matter its riches and rewards, can be worthwhile if a man cannot be honest with himself."

Rajapaksa hustled to reply but could only hang his head in shame. Finally, he raised it and eyed the hordes of wraiths that waited in silence. "Have I done it, then? Is that what you've come to tell me? That it's all my fault? That I am singly responsible for everything that's bad in the nation? That nobody else is at fault and nobody can do anything else? That it was all up to me and I've ruined it?"

A young darkie holding a dead baby in her arms floated forward. Her eyes were hollow as if tears had seared away her eyeballs and the bones around her eye sockets were prongs covered in skin. The sight needled Rajapaksa. Her skin was so dry and tight and emaciated that her ribs poked through her chest. The breasts, long hacked away, had served as somebody's war trophies. Dead nerves waved in frayed tatters where mammary glands had once stood. The baby had been dead a long time and had turned ghostly white. A large gash remained open in the woman's belly, the black blood still fresh and sticky and nauseating. Rajapaksa could just make out the bulge of putrefying intestines, liver, and entrails through the slit.

"My child was untimely ripped out of my belly by Singhalese soldiers, you monster. After they had raped me, this is what they did. And yet, we continue to endure. We continue to continue because we must. What reason do *you* think you have to complain?"

"You faced atrocities on both sides, woman," claimed Rajapaksa. "I could not control what every single boy who fought for me did. Your own fighters did unspeakable things to you but do you speak of them? I came and ended it all. Sometimes one must spill blood to prevent even greater bloodshed. Why do you look at me as if I were the one who had raped you?"

"Do you think that you are the be-all and end-all of our nation?" spat the eyeless wraith. "You are just one in a long line of rapists and motherfuckers to come through. After you're gone, we'll wipe the dirt and the blood from between our legs, stand up and wash ourselves, and continue. You'll be nothing but a dirty memory, a moment of wasted time in an otherwise painful life."

Rajapaksa was taken back by the coldness and fury of her words, the sheer lack of understanding. He startled and looked at his brother. "Dudley, tell this darkie it's not true. Tell her about all the good things I've done."

"Brother, do you remember what you once said to us in private about the burning of the Jaffna library?"

"What did I say?"

"You said that they should be happy they'd no longer have to pay their overdue fines."

"Did I say that?"

"Yes, and they also blame me for what you've done. I can't go anywhere except to lower my head in shame. Don't you have any sensitivity? Any remorse? Can I have looked up to a brother so heartless?"

At this, Rajapaksa finally understood and he wailed inside. Something of the horror finally penetrated his iron-clad heart and he sensed all that had been done, all that could have been, and the very immanent destruction of his soul all around him. How unwise he had been! He had nothing but vaulting ambition to prick the sides of his intent, and now this ambition lay squarely at the centre of his soul. It shattered into a million pieces.

He apologized first to his brother, then to the hordes that stood silently behind him. "I'm sorry. I'm so sorry, brother. Can you find it in yourself to forgive me? It was the lion; it was the lion that got me, that got us all that day at Sigiriya rock... what happened... we could never talk about it. And then what happened again recently. I'm so sorry! It wasn't a lion but some dread spider that laid its sacs of eggs in our mouths that day! We were forever scared as the eggs hatched... would the spiders crawl out or go the other way, down our throats? We never said anything!"

"It was not the lion," chanted the hordes, "nor the tiger."

"Oh please, masters, please, I beg leave of you," pleaded Rajapaksa, turning toward the towering phantasms, "Just give me one more chance! Just give me one more chance and I will make it all better. You will see! I will be a new man! I am transformed by your words, by your leave, by your mercy. Just... give me... one... more... chance... and I will make a new life. A new country!"

With that, his heart almost gave. His body weakened, he collapsed on his knees in the vast entrails of space. The lion and the tiger looked at each other with cold eyes and then nodded with a barely perceptible bristling of the fur. Slowly, very slowly, his brother and the hordes of wraiths disappeared, taking their phantom limbs and too-cruel gashes back into the pot. The tiger loped forward and bit at Rajapaksa's golden spacesuit, his armour. With spectral fangs, the tiger gnashed and soon reduced the small suit to shreds. The lion then approached and the two jungle beasts very tenderly and very delicately, for the charred Rajapaksa was oh so very small, licked the feces and urine off his body. He was like a baby, all shrivelled up. Gone was his belly, his great handlebar of a moustache. He was a completely hairless little being, new and old at the same time.

The lion took this baby in his jaws and picked him up, as if he were the weakest runt of the litter, and nodded to the tiger. The tiger understood wordlessly and retreated into the pot.

Now, only Rajapaksa and the lion were left and the lion carried him away. Slowly, they began their trek down through the four heavens, through time and space and back to the solar system, the small black marble from which Rajapaksa originated.

The waveform of the lion was immune to the hardships and rigours of space but Rajapaksa was not and so, to protect him, the lion took Rajapaksa and swallowed him, devoured him whole. It was strange for Rajapaksa, who had eaten a great many things in life, to be eaten. It was not unpleasant exactly, terrifying, yes, but not unpleasant. The spectral saliva from the lion helped push him through the esophageal tract. Through a process of spectral peristalsis, Rajapaksa was bumped along down the formidable alimentary canal and into the stomach. Gastric metaphysical acids worked at his skin, his eyes, his skull. Slowly, not violently but almost peacefully, Rajapaksa was masticated and digested. His hair had already left him and now the skin and nerves were whittled away. The muscles and sinew were eaten until only his major organs and bones were left. These leathery lungs, this old tired heart, this overworked colon, this sad spongy brain. The last repositories of his personality were soon gone. Rajapaksa was broken down to his essence – a palpable agitated energy – then reconstituted in the lion's tummy. *Is this what it is to be reborn?* wondered Rajapaksa, *To have one's soul broken down then put back together?* He felt small, powerless, insignificant. He was nothing more than a speck of undigested food in the giant being's colon.

So, they travelled like this, through supernovas, skirting black holes, under wormholes and leaping over solar flares, until they finally came back to our solar system and approached Earth. The lion leapt from Venus to Earth in a single bound, carrying Rajapaksa, asleep and healed through the long trip, in his stomach lining as if he were a baby safely tucked within a womb.

The lion burned up as it penetrated Earth's rarefied atmosphere, used to existing as a waveform in space, but it pressed on, sharpening its claws and pressing its nose against the density of air. Waveforms have a short life and an almost mythic sensibility and this particular waveform knew it did not have long to live. All of its will and intent were now focussed on getting Rajapaksa back home and the two burned through re-entry into Earth's atmosphere, like a blazing comet, kissing the ground. Rajapaksa was safe but the waveform burned away, vanished like a dream, dropping him like a flailing stone into the waters of the Nandikadal Lagoon.

*

Rajapaksa came to in the waters and foam, his body covered in slime, and water entering his nostrils. He felt as if he had been thrown forth, vomited into the world anew. He was naked and flailing, did not know whether he would die first through choking or drowning. But at least he was back home! There was the monument that he himself had unveiled to commemorate the winning of the war. There was the boardwalk and railing stretching out over the lagoon. He heaved with breath, drew lungfuls of air into his emaciated husks, those new lungs, let the blood and lymph loose through his body again. After untold time in space, it was good to be back on terra familiar.

He looked down into the water and did not recognize himself. He was naked and pale-skinned. Like an old man, his limbs were spindly, and what little folds of flesh he did retain hung like slices of shaved meat off his ribs. Gone was the large and bounding belly. Gone the many chins and immense thigh flesh. Gone were the glorious moustaches and the jet-black hair. He looked like some starved, hollowed-out Buddhist statue come to life, as if in a fairy tale or fevered dream.

And then Rajapaksa looked up. He knew where he was but did not recognize it. The monument was still there but it was surrounded by netting and a fence; floodlights flanked it and stood by large generators, idle and humming, waiting for the chance to be turned on at night. Large billboard signs were within reading distance at the other side of the lagoon. An advertisement for 'Rajapaxa's Rajaboogies' adorned the huge billboard closest to him and bore a stylized drawing of his own mother with the line 'From Ma Rajapaxa's kitchen to your table,' as if his mother was some sort of Singhalese Aunt Jemima serving pancakes.

His astonishment could not last long for a small navy skiff hovered by to pick him up.

Everything hovered these days, even shopping carts. Rajapaksa could not have known it but while only days had passed for him at close-to-light speed, the rest of the world had trundled on at its own relative slog. Einstein has shown that at speeds close to light, clocks no longer become synchronous and time dilates in immense factors. Dudley had grown old and died. While the lion had journeyed back with Rajapaksa in its maw, its gullet, and then in its stomach, decades had slipped by in the time belonging to old-fashioned Sri Lanka. The world had turned, demagogues and fashions had come and gone, fortunes had risen and fallen, and progress (if we can be charitable enough to call it thus) moved ever forward. It was some eighty years later that Rajapaksa re-entered Earth's atmosphere with nothing but his life. Everybody assumed he had died a long time ago. Even his children had passed on. His grandchildren might be alive somewhere, around, but he would not have known them and could not even guess what they were named.

Still, Sri Lanka is a place steeped in history and tradition and sometimes the old ways are the best ways. There were still Buddhists and Hindus, Singhalese and Tamils, a variety of other groups who came and went, mixed and pulled away. Add to this the first contact between Earth and other sentient life forms which had to inevitably happen and Rajapaksa came back to a whole new world. Sri Lanka, now at war again, had gone from the pearl of South Asia to the slum of South Asia. Decades of war, nepotism, and mismanagement ensured that it was a desirable place for alien refugees fleeing the horrors of their own home planets. Many of these alien refugees built up an idea of Earth and Sri Lanka as a haven from their own terrors, but were sadly surprised to see that things were not much better in the heart of the island. What was worse, most Sri Lankans did not want them there and these aliens lived marginal lives.

With his white hairless body and smooth domed head, the naval officers assumed naturally that Rajapaksa was some alien, a prisoner or a slave, jettisoned from a passing spaceship, that he had stowed away or escaped, that he was an unwanted criminal, yet another parasite preying on the paradise that had once been Ceylon.

They, with their laser guns and navy fatigues, took him south to the interstellar detaining cells at Hambantota spaceport. On the journey there, he saw many things that opened his eyes with wonder and others that made him want to close his eyelids in disgust. Lines of hardened slaves were being marched with glowing LCD necklaces around their necks and arms, in devices like permanent stocks. Rich women and girls floated by in saris that were now so short that they resembled mini-skirts. There seemed to be a huge disparity between the rich who zoomed around on hover bikes and the poor who looked no different from the poor villagers Rajapaksa had bamboozled during his own tenure. And everywhere, he saw the signs: Ma Rajapaxa's secret recipe for Rajaboogies: 'Aliens love 'em! Foreigners love 'em! Sri Lankans can't get enough of 'em! Have some Rajapaxa's Rajaboogies today! Yummy, yummy, yummy for your tummy, tummy, tummy!'

Worst of all, the mighty Buddhist statues and shrines that had once dotted the land had fallen to ruin and disrepair. Some had been raided and scrapped. Once in a while, he recognized a stylized basalt statue of Gota or Hu Jintao that had been erected in place of the old Buddhist ones. But they too had fallen to neglect and ignorance, worn away by acid rain. They had become featureless, like some memory from a time long ago, discoloured and faded in the rain.

Until Rajapaksa caught on to how much time had passed, his first thought had been to journey to the capital and go straight to his brother's house. He would kill Gota and Shiranthi right then and there in their adulterous bed. But this obsession quickly burned away with the understanding that came with it – time had robbed him of even this satisfaction.

Rajapaksa had been reduced from his exalted status to the lowest of the low and he was now no better than a common prisoner. He realized this. He was merely grateful that they had given him a blanket to cover his nakedness, his wrinkled frame, and that they assured him he was not going to be executed or tortured for information.

After he was fed and rested, they brought him into a room to speak to a reassignment officer. The reassigner was white and had a scarred face. He wore a yarmulke.

Though he was very old (ninety?), something of the boy came through. Rajapaksa had a distant memory of a nervy boy selling the big white man a tiny joint, then tucking the bill into his gold sequined change purse and touching it to his forehead. What was his name? What was his *name*!

What is this boy doing speaking Singhalese? wondered Rajapaksa. *What is he even doing here?* The Singhalese language's inflections and idiom had changed in the intervening decades, and the reassigner assumed Rajapaksa had learned the language through language discs on another planet before being smuggled to Earth. The man told him that Sri Lanka was now embroiled in another civil war. The Tamils were again fighting the Singhalese for the same reasons: language, culture, autonomy, revenge. The Tamils were backed by the powerful state of Tamil Nadu in India. India was at war with the Chinese. The Chinese, as of old, backed the Singhalese with weapons and funds. Right now, there was intense fighting in the Palk Strait where both India and China attempted to maintain dominance. They fought bitterly for mobility and control.

Rajapaksa almost wept then as he had wept to Rob Ford, which seemed so long ago, eons, about who he was and what had happened to him but he suspected that the man in front of him would not remember. Surely, if he didn't remember Rob Ford, he remembered the old high school, the green grass in the autumn sun, the cheerleaders jumping up and down! It hit him then that Rob Ford was dead, that probably even the cheerleaders were dead. In fact, everyone he had ever known was dead, and Rajapaksa was utterly alone. The cruel fates had allowed him to live on into a mausoleum of his life, the precious gift of life a bitter pill surrounded by a mouthful of ashes in his throat. Even that tree where Rob Ford and he had carved their names together might no longer be there.

Yet much was the same. Things in Sri Lanka were ever as they were before and Rajapaksa must do something about it. The young man, now an old man, was named Bernie Mandelbaum and a strange sequence of events had brought him to Sri Lanka. Young Bernie had gone on to perform his bar mitzvah splendidly. He went on to graduate high school and became a religious studies scholar at Temple University in Philadelphia. He focused his Ph.D. on anti-Semitism in the Torah and concluded that Jehovah is an anti-Semite.

Young Mandelbaum was then hounded from the university and had to flee for writing things that made other people mad. He ended up in China, teaching English and a little Hebrew on the side. People were eager for English but the Hebrew didn't do so well. Once China made its alliance with the Sri Lankan government and the Sri Lankan state became a vassal to China, it was easy to get a government job on the island. They had stripped government pensions a long time ago so here he was, an old man, working to eke out the last of his days. Rajapaksa tried to tell Mandelbaum about the futility of war, the privations he had endured, the horror he had escaped from just so that he could return and mend his ways. He came with a message from the Gods: repent, repent, repent, mend thy ways before it is all too late!

The reassigner looked at Rajapaksa and nodded his head slowly. He had seen it before: the shock of space travel on lower class freight, what it could do to the brain. Why did they even tolerate these good-for-nothings who just washed up on the shores of their planet with nothing to commend them, nothing to do but suck on the state's resources all day long? Well, if this blubber of a being thought it was an easy ride, he had another thing coming.

Rajapaksa was informed that illegal aliens had two options open to them. Either they could enlist and fight in the service of the new Sri Lankan Army against the rebels or he could work in a government-sponsored factory. Rajapaksa was sick of fighting and anyway, he was too old now. He couldn't imagine picking up a weapon or marching through the arid jungle heat.

He chose the only thing left for him and was assigned to work at the assembly line of Ma Rajapaxa's. This excited him for he hoped that the company was actually run by his descendents and perhaps through hard work and favour or fortuitous circumstance, he might run into them. Then he would tell them stories of his youth and Sri Lanka's past, regale them with tales of their ancestry which, to Rajapaksa, had only happened months ago. Why not? He had been extraordinarily lucky so far. To come from such humble and rootless beginnings to be the prime minister, then president of Sri Lanka... to survive the coldest reaches of space and then return when the rest of his family was dead!

Rajapaksa was assigned to the division that packaged Rajapaxa's Rajaboogies and he worked hard, perhaps harder than he ever had in his entire life. He learned that Rajapaxa's Rajaboogies held a special license from the government to manufacture their snacks throughout the country and then ship them all over the world. The snacks themselves were made out of some kind of strange paste, then moulded into three distinct shapes: a lion, a shawl, and a pair of moustaches. Rajapaksa almost split his sides laughing when he learned the last part. Is this what his legacy and life had finally, finally, been reduced to?

Still, it was good to laugh and he was happy that he could do so. He had always been so stern and serious for photos, for press events, for the role of warlord of the nation. He relished the act of being a humble peasant, being stripped of his armour and his glory, having nothing and expecting nothing from the world.

He never did meet the people who ran the company as almost everyone who worked in his factory were plebes, workers. The highest rank he ever encountered was shift manager. Still, he applied himself to his job with diligence and care though he never ate the snack itself. He had seen kids once eating them on the skybus, enroute to his place of work, and they had speculated what went into them. "They're made of snot," piped one boy, "that's what I heard. Definitely snot."

So Rajapaksa never knew and never enquired as to the secret recipe that produced the paste for Ma Rajapaxa's 'Rajaboogers' and he surmised it must be something like the space food he had once eaten on his flight away from Earth. Cheap and synthetic, disposable but not destructible.

One day, he was asked to go to another plant beside the coast as part of a team of workers to cover for the heavy losses endured by shelling from the rebel forces and the fighting nearby. Rajapaksa went because he had no choice but he was nervous to be so close to the fighting. After they had been let out of the hover lorries and set up in Quonset huts, Rajapaksa's team began their shift. It was a long and hard process to pour the paste into the moulds with the aid of old machines. The machines were always doused by industrial hoses every hour on the dot and Rajapaksa could see why. The paste was not like the space food or a cheap biscuit mixture. It was not even like toothpaste – it was like something else which he knew but could not put his finger upon.

A week later, an army convoy of hover lorries came to the back of the factory. They came in the night and Rajapaksa was the only one awake. He had woken up from one of his feverish dreams in which he saw the weird aunties, or at least heard their cackling laughter.

At first, he thought they had brought workers to relieve him and his compadres and they could finally go back to their home plant. But, with a sinking feeling, Rajapaksa knew this could not be the case. They had not been told anything. He doubted strongly that the workers would not have been given the encouraging news to make them work faster in a country that still vainly called itself socialist. Rajapaksa stood up and got dressed and slowly made his way out of the Quonset hut.

Sometimes, the army personnel had extra rations of authentic tea and good chocolate which they charitably gave out. Rajapaksa made his way to the back of the plant. The night was surprisingly cool and still. He could hear the chirp of the crickets and the boom of the ocean. The only other sound was the roar of the plant furnaces. Something was being poured or melted or changed into something else. A breeze picked up and carried the salt of ocean waves to his nostrils but then he realized there was something else, also salty, also familiar. To his surprise, all the lights had been turned on at the back of the plant and he could see the lights of the furnaces burning away also, the foundry that heated up the paste-processing plant glowing. The convoy of hover vehicles floated there silently and a stream of magnetized pallets came out of them and were ushered by remote control into the factory.

Rajapaksa came closer and looked at the pallets from behind a wall. One had a bent foot peeking out from beneath its grey blanket. A floppy hand lay nearby and he thought of those hordes of phantom wraiths, many of them holding a severed arm or a leg. Another pallet jangled with the airy tinkle of dog tag chains. Yet another showed a pale fingernail growing on a dark finger that continued to grow even after the finger had died.

There was no one watching and so Rajapaksa was able to move forward to get a closer look. He followed the stream of pallets, careful not to get into anyone's line of sight. They floated in and emptied their bodies in a pile in the foundry which now looked like a crematorium. Loose hands were jammed in strangers' mouths. Elbows and knees interlocked. The hair of one man's head nestled into another's genitals. A small boy and a large man looked as if they had their arms around each other in a deathly embrace.

Rajapaksa looked at the large pile of bodies, naked and stripped of all their fatigues and armaments, and tried to puzzle it out. It looked like some strange hundred-headed, thousand-limbed creature. Some demon or rakshasa. A temptation to terrify and abduct the mendicant on his path to enlightenment.

And then enlightenment hit Rajapaksa. It came like a diamond bullet right through his forehead. He knew what they were. He knew exactly what Rajapaxa's Rajaboogies was made out of. It was not snot, nor brains, nor skin, nor lymph, nor sinew. It was all of these.

"Oh, my God!" screamed Rajapaksa in total horror and awareness, "Rajapaksa's Rajaboogies is people!"

Acknowledgements

I would like to thank the Ontario Arts Council's Writers' Reserve Grants for providing assistance towards the completion of this project.

Thanks to Luc & John and Maddy & Sarah.

Thanks also to Amarnath, Nancy, Viranjith, Anne, and Kumaran.

In memory of my dear friend, Pete Cram.

*

To follow Koom Kankesan's writing, join:

http://www.facebook.com/KoomKankesanThePanicButton?fref=ts